Voice From the Grave

Then Anna saw the other grave, read the stone, and felt the hair rise on the back of her neck.

"Was this for me?" she gasped aloud. "Am I supposed to be buried here?" She read the stone again, more carefully.

> This grave lies waiting for our dearly beloved child, Hanna

Waiting!
Waiting for my body!
The moaning wind behind her carried a voice from a grave. "No, child, no. Waiting for you to come back through it."

Also by Larry Weinberg

Don't Look in the Mirror

Escape from Ghost Hotel

Hunted!

Return to Ghost Hotel

Shivers and Shakes

GHOST HOTEL

Larry Weinberg

Rainbow Bridge®
Troll

This edition published in 2001.

LIBRARY OF CONGRESS CATALOGING-IN-PUBLICATION DATA
Weinberg, Larry.
  Ghost hotel / by Larry Weinberg.
    p.   cm.
    Summary: Mysteriously drawn to an Indiana museum, a twelve-
year-old paralyzed girl encounters ghosts who return her to a former
life, where she attempts to save the son of a freed slave traveling by
Underground Railroad in Kentucky.
  ISBN 0-8167-3420-8 (pbk.)
  [1. Ghosts—Fiction.   2. Time travel—Fiction.   3. Slavery—
Fiction.   4. Fugitive slaves—Fiction.   5. Underground railroad—
Fiction.   6. Abolitionists—Fiction.   7. Afro-Americans—Fiction.]
I. Title.
PZ7.W4362Gh   1994
[Fic]—dc20   94-2970

Published by Rainbow Bridge, an imprint and registered
trademark of Troll Communications L.L.C.

Printed in Canada.

To Janie, who travels through time at my side.

ONE

They had been driving all day. Now it was nighttime. Wind and an angry rain from a late summer storm whipped the rented minivan. The country road was dark and lonely, and lined with nothing but trees. There were no lights from houses anywhere, the windshield wipers had stopped working suddenly, and the Post family was lost.

Anna thought there was enough excitement going on without telling her adoptive family—father, mother, and little brother—what was happening to her. For some time now she'd been feeling as if electricity was going through her body. It was a tingling that had started in those paralyzed legs of hers shortly after they'd crossed over the bridge from Kentucky into Indiana. For some crazy reason she couldn't figure out, Anna felt that some incredible change in her was about to take place. And it grew stronger and stronger as the minivan splashed along through the pitch black night.

The Posts had never been to Indiana before, yet with every passing moment Anna was surer that somehow she knew exactly where they were. The feeling was in the back of her mind, so close. . . .

Suddenly the sky turned white—and Anna saw it. The house was exactly as it had been in her dreams. "We passed it! We just passed it."

"Passed what, hon?" Her unhappy father sighed at the wheel. "A motel?"

"No. Well, maybe like a . . . a hotel. It's off the road, up behind the trees."

From her seat next to her husband in front, Mrs. Post had been staring hard at thick dark woods on both sides of the narrow road. "Where? I didn't see anything."

"Back there on the right, Mom. I saw it when the lightning flashed."

"Anna, there wasn't any lightning. You must have been dozing. Let's keep going, Allan, till we find that town you were so anxious to visit—or at least *some* town. I really don't see why we had to come here after all these days of dragging ourselves over every Civil War battlefield in Virginia, Tennessee, and Kentucky. Practically nobody has ever even heard about a battle in Indiana."

"Well there *was* one. A Confederate general marched in with a couple thousand men. And what excites me about it is that it was ordinary farmers, not soldiers, who fought them and drove—"

Anna was starting to panic. She felt as if her big chance—for something—was being lost. "Hey, Kevin," she suddenly blurted to her brother. "How's it going? Still managing to hold it in?"

For the last half hour her brother had been bent over, clutching his sides in painful silence. Now he moaned. "I've got to go to the bathroom!"

Mrs. Post whirled around in her seat and shot an angry look at her daughter. "You had to start him up when there's nothing that can be done about it?"

"But he *can* go, Mom. In that place we passed."

"I'm telling you there was nothing—"

"Peace!" cried Mr. Post wearily, and everyone fell silent. "Okay, we'll check it out."

The minivan turned around. In a few minutes its headlights were shining on a flapping wooden sign that read Terwilliger Inn. There was another sign nailed into an old oak tree. But in all the rain and darkness—and with the wind slapping a leafy branch against it—someone would have had to get out to read what the sign said.

"*Terwilliger*," Anna repeated to herself. It almost meant something to her. But what? She felt her heart begin to race. Her father, rather than waste any more time looking at signs, started the car up the narrow dirt road.

The building was several stories high, with curved walls and little balconies. "It looks lovely," Mrs. Post said softly as they parked. "Very old, but so well kept up. I wonder why there are no lights."

"Because everyone here is dead," mumbled Anna without realizing what she had said.

"*Dead?*" shrieked Kevin. "Mommy, she's trying to scare me!"

Mrs. Post glared at her. "Anna! Why do you insist on tormenting him?"

"I don't! It just slipped out wrong. I meant to say that everybody's in bed."

"Makes sense," Mr. Post said quickly. "The storm must have knocked out the electricity."

Anna felt a bit guilty for scaring Kevin. Not that the kid didn't deserve it. He had been annoying her a good deal lately, jumping ahead of her into the wheelchair and claiming that he couldn't walk either. Or lying stretched out in bed when it was time to get up and saying he'd forgotten how to stand. He acted as if not being able to walk was some kind of joke.

While Mrs. Post hurried with the little boy up the wide marble steps to the big porch, Anna's father went around to the back door of the van to take down her wheelchair. By the time he got it down, though, Anna was already trying to come through the side door by herself.

"Hey, wait up," he said. "What do you think you're doing?"

"Dad, I'm almost sure I can make it on my own," she cried excitedly as her feet swung outside. "I feel as if I used to walk up those steps all the time. Please let me try!"

Mr. Post stood there in the drenching rain, staring at her. "This is getting a bit crazy. You know that?"

"Yes! It's crazy for me, too. But I just want to try to walk. No, no! Don't take my arm." She took one half step, twisted . . . and before she could hit the ground, fell into her father's arms.

"My sweet baby, I'm sorry," he murmured in her ear. "But just keep working at those parallel bars back home and you'll get it sometime, I promise you."

After helping her into the wheelchair, he pulled it backward up the steps. They caught up with the rest of the family in the lobby. Kevin was looking desperate, but the darkness and the stillness brought them all to a halt. Mr. Post took a little penlight out of his pocket and flicked it on. He walked to the polished mahogany front desk where there was a bell and rang it several times.

Silence.

"How old fashioned!" said Mrs. Post, looking about at the white wicker furniture, the high windows, the sloping roof far above their heads.

"And what a find!" agreed her husband enthusiastically. "It's right out of my favorite time."

Mrs. Post shook her head at her husband. "Sometimes I think you wished you'd lived back then. Well, nobody's coming. You'd better give me that flashlight, Allan, before our son has an accident."

Taking her suffering boy by the hand, she hurried off with him into a corridor.

Anna stayed with her father. "Dad, I want to know what you think."

Mr. Post shrugged. "Well, I guess you said it right. With the lights out, it means that everybody went to bed."

"No, I mean about something else."

"What?"

"Forget it. It's dumb."

"I seriously doubt that," he said gently. "Tell me."

"I'm . . . uh . . . I'm not ready. So . . . you think this house goes back to the Civil War?"

"Well, I'd say it was built a bit before that. Say maybe fifteen, twenty years earlier, in the days of Huck Finn and Tom Sawyer. There were paddleboats on the Mississippi in those days. Some of them would steam all the way up it till they reached that river we crossed a while ago, the Ohio. This hotel can't be too far from the waterfront. I wouldn't be surprised if a lot of the early guests didn't come that far by boat, then hop into a stagecoach or a buggy and drive out here."

Anna gazed at her father in wonderment. "You can tell all that just standing here in the dark, Dad?"

Mr. Post smiled. "Just letting my imagination roam."

She gave a sharp little laugh, and started to bring up what was really on her mind. "Want to hear what *my* imagination tells me?"

"Sure."

"It's telling me that I know this place. I've been here before."

"Not surprising, when I'm always talking about American history to you. I'm sure you've had your share of dreams about log cabins and covered wagons, too."

Anna frowned. "No, Dad. I'm not talking about dreams."

Her father seemed to tighten up and grow unsure of himself. She could feel it even in the darkness. "What then?" he asked in a husky voice. "You're saying you've been here before—for real?"

Anna hesitated. She didn't really know how to answer. Maybe this *was* crazy.

"Honey," he said gently, "this is an awfully long way—I would guess at least five hundred miles—from that old abandoned farm where we found you. But I suppose it's possible. I'll tell you what. Tomorrow we'll look around here carefully. Just remember that you've had feelings like this before, of recognizing places or faces."

"Not this strong, Dad."

Mr. Post began to whistle "The Battle Hymn of the Republic." He had a habit of doing that whenever he needed to calm himself. Anna remained silent until at last he said, "Well, let's hope it really works out this time."

He had spoken honestly and his voice had even been cheerful, but Anna could still tell that he was feeling shaky. "What's so familiar about it?" he asked her.

"I . . . I don't know. I'm not sure. The outside of it, I guess."

"So, can you describe the inside? What the rest of the place looks like?"

"No, I . . . Dad, it's hard when I try to force myself."

"Just take it easy then. What's the first thing that comes into your mind?"

"I dunno. Well . . . maybe a tunnel . . . I guess." Anna grew anxious. "I know that sounds weird!"

"Not necessarily. Plenty of old houses have tunnels. Back in colonial times people used them to hide from Indian war parties and get to the stockades, where the ammunition was kept. Some of the same tunnels were used much later to hide runaway slaves from the South. And some people in the Underground Railroad built new ones."

Suddenly Anna was filled with worry and confusion. "Tell me the truth, Dad. Will it ever come back to me—who I really am and who my birth parents are?"

"Yes, I think it's going to happen," Mr. Post said reassuringly. "You know why?"

"Why?"

"Because you've grown three years older and a lot

stronger inside. You're better able to deal with the memory of whatever it was that horrified you so much that you had to block out everything from your past."

"And . . . and will I be able to walk then?"

"Maybe." Anna heard her father sigh. "No one can promise you that, but I think it's very possible. There was nothing in the x rays the doctors took after we found you that showed anything wrong with your legs. And the psychologist thought that what you went through must have made you feel very helpless—so helpless that you somehow became convinced you couldn't even *try* to run away. But you've heard all this before."

"Yes, sure; but Dad, I *did* run away from something. And I think that there was something I had to do but I didn't, because I was too afraid to turn around. I was a coward!"

"What a ridiculous name to call yourself, Anna. There isn't anyone who hasn't been afraid, or run from something because it was much too scary for them to deal with."

Just then Mrs. Post returned with a much happier Kevin. "We left a little mess in the bathroom because the plumbing doesn't work, what with the electricity being out. But other than that the place is wonderful! We just found the most darling set of rooms that no one is using. Big brass beds and lovely antique furniture. Don't you think it makes sense to stay here for the night? We could leave a note on the desk saying that we'll register and pay in the morning."

"Anna has a feeling about this place, Barb. She thinks she's been here before."

The smile on Mrs. Post's face faded. "Do you believe that?"

Her husband shrugged. "It's always possible, since none of us knows where she really comes from. But I suppose it's more likely there's something about it that reminds her of someplace else. And if that's the case, it could help bring up some connections." He offered a little smile in the dark.

"Yes, I suppose so," said Anna's mother. "But I don't want to see her disappointed. We've had what we thought were leads before. It's always been so miserable for her when they don't turn out."

"I can handle that, Mom."

"And I believe her," said Mr. Post.

"Daddy, you believe *everything* she says!" Kevin snorted. "Even when she's lying!"

His sister wheeled around on him. "Shut up, Kev. I'm just like George Washington. I never lie."

"That's a lie, too!" he snapped back, shining the penlight in her face.

Mrs. Post was fed up. "I've had three endless weeks of eating, sleeping, and breathing the Civil War between the North and the South. I want the war between the children in my family to stop!"

Mr. Post made the mistake of thinking he was changing the subject when he said, "I was telling Anna that this place must have been a hotel even before the war."

His wife took a very long, deep breath and started again in as patient a tone as she could manage. "Allan . . . darling . . . I love you to pieces, but give—it—a—rest."

At this point her husband began to whistle "The Battle Hymn of the Republic" again.

Everyone stared at him. "He doesn't know that he's doing it, Mom," Anna said quietly.

"I know, I know." Mrs. Post sighed. "Allan, will you go get our bags, please? Then let's all take off these wet things and get to bed. There will be plenty of time to find out about this place in the morning."

TWO

When Anna woke, the first rays of sunlight were showing through the white curtains that covered the windows. She was still a little sleepy, but Kevin—probably the only six-year-old in the world who could snore!—was in the next bed, sounding like a chain saw.

Lying there staring at the ceiling, she wondered what had made this place seem so familiar to her last night. Looking around, she saw that there was absolutely nothing about this room that told her a thing, although she did notice that there were no lights to turn on here. Unless she counted that big candle in a dish. Now *that* was pretty weird.

Leaning over the side of the bed, Anna pulled her clothes from the suitcase and struggled into them. Then wriggling, pushing, and sliding, she dumped herself into the wheelchair and headed off to do some exploring.

As she wheeled down the corridor, her watch said it was only six forty-five, but there was already an old couple in the lobby. They seemed to fit in with a hotel that apparently had no use for electricity. Anna couldn't help staring at them.

A frilly lace cap covered the woman's graying hair, and a long plain dress reached down to her ankles. She wore old-fashioned eyeglasses as she sat in an armchair, knitting. The man was tall and had a great head of snow white hair and a big drooping mustache. There was no arm inside the left sleeve of his long blue jacket, and he stood very straight, like those photographs of old officers she'd seen in her dad's Civil War picture books. He wore a jacket that was very long in the back, and had a big fluffy bow tie on a shirt that came up above the top of his neck. He was standing by a huge stone fireplace, puffing on a pipe. As Anna entered, he took it from his mouth and pointed it at her.

"Ah," he said warmly. "Somebody who came in during the storm last night! Welcome to the Terwilliger Inn, young lady. We are your hosts. Do say hello to her, Dora."

The old lady looked up from her knitting. "A visitor, how nice! But this light is so dim. And my eyesight isn't too good anymore, even with these spectacles. So why don't you come over here, child, and let me take a better look at you. My, what a bright and perky face! How old are you, if I may ask?"

"Twelve," said Anna, wheeling the chair toward her. She wondered now if these people belonged to some special group, like the Amish, who tried to keep to old-time ways and didn't even drive cars. Her father had talked about them when they visited the battlefield at Gettysburg last year, although most of them lived in a different part of Pennsylvania.

"Do you still go to school?"

"Of course." Anna was surprised by the question. These people couldn't be *that* much out of it, could they?

"Wonderful! In my day most girls your age were just expected to stay home and do the chores. Now I do hope you will stay on and finish your studies."

"I will."

"Good," said the old woman. But the smile on her face seemed to have frozen and her knitting needles had stopped clicking.

Anna grew edgy under her searching gaze. "Forgive me," the woman apologized, noticing Anna's unease. "I just can't help staring at you. Your voice and your face remind me so of someone. But, of course, it's so easy to make a mistake. Especially when a good deal of time has gone by since last I saw her."

A look of great sadness passed over the old woman's face like a cloud, and she lowered her head. "It was in this very room. We—the colonel and I— have been hoping ever since that she"—the woman's voice broke—"that she would return to us."

Anna felt the prickle of goose bumps. And her legs were beginning to tingle with the same electric feeling that had shot through her yesterday. She didn't recall asking, "Who was she?" yet the colonel replied as if she had.

"Our little girl," he said heavily. "Alas, she was only nine when she disappeared. At first we thought she had been murdered, but my wife consulted someone who told her an incredible thing. Of course, I did not believe it then. I refused to have anything to do with anyone who claimed to be able to look beyond the grave. But this person—they called her the Conjure Woman—claimed that our daughter's spirit could not be found among the dead. She told my wife that our child had escaped her pursuers by— what were her words, Dora?"

"She skipped ahead, Amos." The old woman exchanged glances with her husband. "Do you believe it now?"

"We mustn't jump to conclusions, dearest. And for her sake as well as our own, we need to be cautious. It has been so very long."

"I . . . I don't understand," said Anna, feeling the electric tingling growing stronger.

"Who does understand God's miracles, child? Our Hanna leaped ahead into another place, another time. And we have been hoping she would come back to us ever since. Until we see her again just once, we will never rest."

"Won't you tell us your name?" the woman asked.

"Anna."

"So close! So close!" the old woman exclaimed, and her hand went fluttering to her chest.

Anna felt a shiver go up her back. It was beginning to dawn on her that these people might be crazy.

The man must have noticed that Anna was uneasy. "This is our hotel and you are most welcome," he said quickly. "Our name is Terwilliger. Dora and Amos. And your parents are . . . ?"

"Allan and Barbara Post," Anna said nervously. "We're from Rochester, New York."

"Rochester," repeated the old man, as if there was something about the name that amazed him. Suddenly, his dark eyes seemed to light up. "Of course! The *Posts*!" He turned excitedly to his wife. "Dora, you remember Isaac and Amy Post. Their house in Rochester was the main stopping place for the slaves before the final dash to Canada. The Posts were wonderful. What brave fighters they were! Not only for freedom for all races but for the rights of women, too!"

Anna stared hard at the old man. The grandparents of her dad's grandparents had helped to run the Underground Railroad before the Civil War. Amos Terwilliger was talking about them as if he'd known them personally!

Anna started backing away. "Listen," she said in as friendly a voice as she could manage, "I think I'd better get my folks. I know they'd like to talk to you about—"

But no one was fooled. "One question, child!" shouted the old woman before Anna could wheel herself into the corridor. "Are they your *real* parents? Or did you come to them only three years ago?"

Anna's hands froze. So they *did* know her! And yet . . . and yet . . . What was wrong with her? Why wasn't she shouting for joy? What was making her feel so strange?

"Child, please turn around," pleaded the old woman.

"Dora, look what we are doing to her. We have seen her and that is enough. Now we must go. We must go."

"But I can't! Not after all these years of waiting and not knowing."

"That is not a good reason, Dora. Not now, when she has so clearly forgotten who we are."

"But she *came* to us. *Something* must have brought her here."

"Your own longings, dearest. *You* drew her here. If it was God's will that a miracle saved her from those slave-hunting murderers, then He willed her to an entirely new life. What right do we have to disturb it? Let us be grateful that she has many years ahead of her. It is obvious that she is loved and cared for—and by descendants of the Posts, no less, people who were with us in the same struggle. Let us take solace in that and return to our resting places."

"What?" cried the old woman frantically. "I could not take her in my arms *then*! Am I not to do it *now*?"

"Dora, that would not ever be possible."

"You don't know that, Amos. I sit in this chair, I touch this knitting."

The old man tried to lower his voice so that Anna could not hear him. "My dearest, look around us. The sun is starting to flood this room. Already we are things of fright to her. Ghosts! Should the last sound we ever hear be the voice of our child screaming in horror?"

Anna, whose ears were sharp, had heard every word he said. She saw the old woman lift a hand to a beam of sunlight. The shaft was passing right through it! She turned her head a bit more, and her eyes bulged in astonishment. The Terwilligers were growing as transparent as glass.

"Look at her, Dora. She knows now what we are."

An icy blast ran though Anna's body. She'd been talking to dead people! Ghosts. These were *ghosts*!

"She knows *what* we are," repeated the old woman with passion. "Then, Amos, we must tell her *who we were*."

Silence. The colonel coughed. And Anna, in spite of her terror, gritted her teeth and swung fully around to face them. She knew what they would say.

"You were our Hanna, our only child," the old woman began softly. "We lived and died long ago. We were your parents, and we loved you with all our hearts. Come, Amos."

Taking each other by the arm, the fading old couple turned to go.

Moving swiftly, Anna followed them to the porch. "Wait! Don't leave."

They had reached the bottom of the stairs and were walking—no, they were floating now—across the lawn. "Oh, please," Anna called out, "you can't go now! I need you to tell me about myself!"

A faint voice came back to her. "Your father was right. We have put terror in your heart."

"No!" she shouted as forcefully as she could.

The colonel called back in an even fainter voice. "We thank you for that noble lie, Hanna. Farewell."

"Okay! All right! I'm scared to death! But you don't understand. I know there's something I have to do. Something I have to change. And it can't happen until I . . . Oh, please, please, can't you stay and help me to remember?"

She could barely see them now, but it seemed to Anna that the spirits of Colonel and Mrs. Terwilliger had stopped moving. They flickered, as if they were struggling to keep from vanishing. In the midst of this, speaking so softly that Anna could not be sure whose voice it was—or whether she had only heard it in her mind—one of them asked, "You are sure you wish for this?"

They were turning to look at her. They were waiting.

Anna took a deep, shaky breath. Could she really handle what might be coming? She waited until her trembling had almost stopped. Then quietly she said, "Yes."

And the ghosts, growing more visible now, slowly came back across the lawn. Gripping her chair so hard that her fingers hurt, Anna watched their feet touch down upon the steps. Watched them come closer and closer until they stood before her.

"May I . . . may I try to touch you?" asked the old woman, lifting her ghostly arm.

Despite the shudder that ran straight up Anna's back, she held still while the wrinkled and transparent hand came up to her face. It brushed her skin so lightly that it felt as if only a breeze had caressed it.

It was a touch and it wasn't a touch. And perhaps because Anna, too, really wanted so much more, her eyes grew hot behind her burning tears.

THREE

This is what Allan Post remembered about his daughter's disappearance. It is what he explained to the chief of police as they all sat in the lobby after Anna's mother frantically drove into town to get help.

He'd been sleeping when Anna came into the room to wake him and Barbara. Still groggy, he'd only half listened when Anna explained something about an old couple she'd met in the lobby who wanted to show her around. But they had to leave very soon—so would it be all right if she went with them now?

Barbara Post remembered asking who they were. "Oh, they're two very nice old people," Anna had said.

The chief, who had been taking notes silently, looked up at them. "You're sure she didn't tell you their names?" he asked with a frown.

Mrs. Post jumped to her feet, very angry with herself. "I'm sure. And it was stupid of us not to ask."

Gritting his teeth, her husband nodded. "I could just kick myself for letting Anna talk me out of going with her. She thought they could help her figure out what was so familiar about this hotel because they knew so much about it. I said, 'Wait up and I'll get dressed and meet them.' But she just kissed me and said, 'Dad, you

29

can hardly keep your eyes open. Go back to sleep. If anything interesting turns up, I'll come back for you.' Well, I was so beat from all that driving last night—Barb and I both were—we both just conked right out again. But if she's been kidnapped—"

"Allan, don't even say it!"

The chief held up a hand. "Let's keep calm, folks, please, and not jump to any conclusions."

"Yes, but look at the situation!" Allan cried. "There was no reason for any people at all to be here, not even us. We didn't find out until after she was gone that this hasn't been a hotel in God knows how long. There was so much wind and rain last night that we hadn't read the other sign at the bottom of the road, the one that said it was a historical site, a kind of museum. Barbara first took a look at it when she drove out of here to get hold of you. But you just said a few minutes ago that the museum is only open to visitors during the day. If that's true, why wasn't it locked last night?"

"I can't say yet, Mr. Post. Maybe the caretaker forgot to shut it. But now let's deal with these people. Did you see another car outside when you arrived?"

"No. But it could have been around the back. Or they could have arrived here after us."

"Allan, why would anybody take Anna?"

"I don't know! Why does *anyone* do anything crazy?"

"What else *did* your daughter say about them?"

Barbara paused to think. "Wait a minute, Allan. Didn't she tell you that the colonel reminded her of you, because he was interested in history? He'd even heard about those people in your family who were in the Underground Railroad."

The chief looked up from his notes, a strange glint in his eyes. "Your daughter said the man was a *colonel*? And he knew all about the Underground Railroad?"

"That's right," said Allan, suddenly hopeful. "Do you have an idea who he is?"

"Well, yes and no."

"What the heck does *that* mean?"

The chief took a long breath before answering. "You might not like what I'm going to suggest. But—"

Just then a young police officer who had been going over the grounds outside came into the lobby and called the chief aside. Watching the two men mutter between themselves made Anna's parents even more jittery, but when the chief turned back to them, he looked a bit relieved.

"Folks, there are some tracks outside that could have been made by the wheelchair. No footprints, though, I'm glad to say. Because you're right, I *was* worried about a kidnapping. For now let's leave your son where he is with my man in the squad car and see if we can't find your daughter together."

The Posts hurried outside and onto the great lawn.

The younger officer went ahead, brushing aside the uncut grass as he carefully examined the ground.

The wheelchair marks led them down a very long slope toward a clump of trees and overgrown bushes, behind which was a small abandoned cemetery.

"When you were looking for her before," the chief asked them, "did you go down as far as the graves?"

Allan shook his head. "She wouldn't have gone there. Anna hates graveyards."

"Uh-huh. It looks as if she went to this one, though."

Cupping her hands in front of her mouth, Barbara shouted, "Anna! Where are you? Are you there? Are you hurt?"

There was no answer.

There was no one in the tiny cemetery and nothing to see but very old gravestones. Many had fallen down long ago. Most of those that remained standing were so worn that it was hard to make out what was written on them. But the chief, leading the way, seemed to know exactly where he wanted to take them. Stopping before a particular stone, he waited until the Posts caught up to him and then pointed to the writing. "I'd like you to read what it says."

"I don't get this," Allan protested.

"For goodness' sake, can't you just do it?" cried Barbara impatiently. "Never mind, I will!"

"'Colonel Amos Terwilliger,'" she read aloud, and then stopped to wipe away a splattering of mud with her fingers before she could make out the rest. "'Born 1801, died 1883. Patriot. Hero of the War to Save the Union. Beloved husband and father.'"

Barbara looked up at the chief. "What's the point? That the man was a colonel?"

"Please just read the one next to it," suggested the chief patiently.

Barbara read: "'Dora Terwilliger. 1804–1891. Abolitionist. Freer of slaves. Faithful wife and mother.'"

"Now listen, folks," said the chief. "I know this will sound off base to you, but hear me out to the end. For a bunch of years before the Civil War, the Terwilligers were very active in the Underground Railroad. They ran this place as a hotel, but they also hid runaway slaves inside."

"But what's the connection?" asked Allan.

"My guess is that Colonel and Mrs. Terwilliger are the same people your daughter said were going to show her around."

Allan Post stared at the man as if the police officer had gone mad. "Oh now, *come on!*"

"You said you'd hear me out. Now I want you to read the headstone on that little grave behind these two."

The Posts read it together in silence.

THIS GRAVE LIES WAITING FOR OUR DEARLY BELOVED CHILD, HANNA. BORN 1841. DIED 1850. BY SLAVE HUNTERS SOMEWHERE CRUELLY MURDERED.

"The girl's body was never found," declared the chief. "But her mother went a little crazy and used to come to this empty grave every day to mourn. There's a story that says eventually she went to see one of those folks who say they can speak to the dead. When she couldn't find the girl among the dead, the spiritualist told Mrs. Terwilliger that her child was still alive. According to the story, she said the child had *skipped ahead* to another place and time. Afterward Mrs. Terwilliger swore never to rest until she saw her Hanna again."

Allan Post glared at him. "What is the point of this? My wife and I are worried sick, and you're trying to get us to believe that *ghosts* have lured our daughter off with them into the land of the dead?"

The chief held up a hand. "Not at all. Personally, I don't believe in that stuff. In my opinion either your daughter knew about this legend before you came here, or she found some old magazine article about the Terwilligers lying around in the lobby."

Allan was ready to explode. "You're absolutely wrong if you think our Anna is hiding somewhere, letting us go through this torment just to get back at us for something. She is not that kind of child. She would never play such a vicious trick!"

"Well, of course, you know her and I don't," said the chief carefully. "But I am a police officer and I can tell you for a fact that even the best of kids can be a little heartless some—"

"She would never do a thing like that!" shouted Mrs. Post, too agitated to notice that she was stepping on Hanna Terwilliger's grave.

The chief frowned. "Well, then, the alternative is that she bought into the legend and convinced herself she was seeing them. Maybe she even believes she's the missing Hanna. There are enough points of similarity, you know. Their first names, Hanna and Anna, are very close. Mrs. Post, you told me on the way here that she's an adopted child who suffers from amnesia. And her age when you found her—"

"But this child died over a hundred and forty years ago!" cried Allan. "Our daughter would have to be crazy to convince herself that she's the same person!"

"Look, like I said before, I don't know her. But I've got to tell you that I'm an adopted child myself. I had no knowledge about my real parents, and when I was about Anna's age, I certainly did a lot of wild daydreaming about who I was and . . ."

Mrs. Post was barely listening. Over the last few hours a gusting wind had blown a good deal of loose brush down to the bottom of the hill, where the little cemetery lay. As she moved around nervously, she accidentally stepped in front of Hanna Terwilliger's gravestone. Twigs cracked underneath her right foot. Then her leg disappeared into the earth and she sank in to her knee.

The police chief leaped forward and pulled her free.

35

"Move back, both of you," he ordered. He bent over and cleared away more of the opening. It was round, and wide enough to hold a body.

"On second thought," he said, reaching for his flashlight, "maybe you two ought to go back to the house and wait."

"Allan, she's dead! I know it. Our baby is dead!"

Post grabbed his wife and shook her. "Stop talking like that, Barbara. We can't let ourselves think that."

The chief shone his light into the opening. "It's empty, thank God. For a minute I was afraid that . . . "

When he didn't finish his thought, Allan screamed at him. "Afraid that what? That she'd climbed inside of it and *killed* herself? Or that the Terwilligers *shoved* her into it?"

"Chief." The young officer, who had gone off into the bushes, suddenly called out. "Can you come here?"

Warning the Posts not to follow him, the chief hurried off. Allan and Barbara held each other tightly as they waited.

"She isn't here either," the police officer called back to them after an agonizing moment. "But we did find this."

And the young officer, being very careful not to destroy any fingerprints, lifted Anna Post's wheelchair into the air.

FOUR

The ghosts had asked Anna to come with them. There was so little time before they would lose strength and fade away. And there was much to show her, both inside and outside of the hotel.

She had hurried off to tell her parents not to worry. She planned to lie to them and say only that she was going to do a little looking around on her own. Instead she'd found herself chattering about the "nice old couple" she had found in the lobby. Not a word about what was really going on—that the Terwilligers were ghosts who claimed to be her real parents. That was crazy, because it meant that she, like they, had lived in the distant past!

Of course, she knew why she hadn't told them everything. Mom and Dad would have thought something was terrifically wrong with her and would have refused to let her leave their room. Or else they would have run out into the lobby themselves. And if they did, she was practically certain that the Terwilligers would have vanished.

Still in all, when Anna guided her wheelchair back toward the lobby, she almost hoped they'd no longer be there.

But there they were, although a bit harder to see.

"One thing has not changed in all this time," said the colonel with admiration. "You still have a great deal of courage."

"I hope that's what it is, and not something else," Anna said ruefully. "So okay, what's on the program?"

"Come, Hanna," said Dora Terwilliger, gliding rather than stepping behind the hotel manager's desk.

Anna followed until she came to a closed door. The colonel moved past them and tried to turn the knob. It moved slightly, but that wasn't enough. Anna turned it and they went through.

They entered a short corridor. There were rooms on either side of it, but not very big ones, judging by how close together the doors were.

"Until shortly before you were born," explained Mrs. Terwilliger, "we had this whole huge house to ourselves and lived upstairs. These were the servants' rooms. Then we lost most of our money, but even so, we were all quite happy here until the day . . . "

The old woman's voice had grown shaky, and then it broke off.

"Until the day that we lost you, Hanna," said the colonel, his mustache twitching as he completed his wife's thought. "You remember nothing?"

Anna paused before another closed door. "What's in there?"

"It's the room where you were born," Mrs.

Terwilliger said eagerly. "And where I used to sing to you when you were very small. Close your eyes, Hanna, just for a moment."

As Anna did so, she heard:

> "Blow, blow
> Sweet and low
> Wind of the western sea-ee."

The singing seemed to come, not from the old woman next to her, but from inside the room. For a moment it even seemed that the voice was much younger, happier.

Anna pushed open the door and went inside. She was surrounded by children's things: crib, toys, a dressing table, a little desk, and a bigger bed.

"It's beautiful here," she said with feeling, and then grew silent.

"But you don't remember anything, do you?" the Terwilligers asked together.

Anna shook her head. Moving to the dresser, she picked up a box with a carving of a tiny blue horse on top. As she opened the lid, the box began to play the same song Mrs. Terwilliger had just been singing. Anna sighed, feeling terrible for these ghosts, and perhaps for herself, as well. Moving over to the cradle, which stood near a stone fireplace, she pushed it and listened to the creak.

"Your father made that out of hickory wood just before I gave birth to you," said Dora Terwilliger. "It was wintertime, and I wove the little quilt. Often, though, I moved you into our room and slept beside you."

Anna ran her hands over the soft wool blanket. Dust rose from it.

"I nursed you," said the ghost of Mrs. Terwilliger in a voice that sounded as if she were forcing herself to be hopeful. "I had wanted so badly to do that myself. Where I was born, down in Kentucky, a woman who came from money might be too proud of her figure. She'd have a slave mother do it. A slave nursed me. I loved her so. But after all my brothers and sisters were too old to take her milk, my parents had no more use for her and they sold her. I tell you, child, I felt so sorry for her. And for myself, too, because I never saw her again. That's when I first began to realize that there was something terribly wrong with slavery. People who were trapped in it were not treated as human beings. And I saw so many examples of how cruel that was that—"

"Dora," said her husband's ghost gently. "I think you're losing sight of what we're trying to accomplish here."

"Yes, you're right. I have been rattling on. But, oh, Amos, here is where I fed her . . . and dressed her . . . and taught her to read. It's a room where she lived for nine long years, yet she doesn't recall a thing about it."

"So what else have you got to show me before you people fade away in one direction and I fade in another?" Anna demanded in a voice that was sharper than she'd intended.

They stared at her. "You are angry with us," said the colonel.

"No, I'm—well, maybe I am!"

"But why?"

"Because you're telling me all this and nothing is changing! I don't remember one bit of it! Is there anything else for me to see . . . or know . . . that might help me remember?" Tears of frustration formed in her eyes.

The colonel grew thoughtful. Then he said, "We could show you the crawl tunnel and the secret room where the fugitives were hidden. You spent some time down there, teaching Little Rafe what you knew about reading and writing."

"Who was Little Rafe?"

"Mrs. Sims's child."

"And who was Mrs. Sims?"

"Rosalie Sims," said Dora. "She'd been a slave on the other side of the river, down in Kentucky. But then we bought her freedom and she came to work for us here in Indiana, where slavery wasn't allowed. She became my friend, and I tried to help her find her

41

little boy. Rafe had been taken from her arms and sold a few years before. Once we started looking for him, we decided to help other slaves escape, too. We had to do it in secret, naturally, but Rosalie took most of the risks. She was called Mother Freedom by the slaves, and their masters learned to hate her. When they finally discovered who she was, they sent men across the river to kill her. It happened a few days after we rescued her little boy. We were hiding him, because a law had been passed that said fugitives had to be returned to their owners. Rosalie was trying to save him from being recaptured and carried back south when slave catchers shot her."

Anna felt a stabbing pain in her heart, as if Rosalie's death had occurred only yesterday. Her brain was whirling. "When did all of this happen?"

"It was in 1850. You were nine years old."

"Wait a minute. You mean we're talking about even *before* the Civil War?"

"Yes, eleven years before. And if Rosalie hadn't been murdered, she could have saved so many more slaves from having to wait until emancipation! Child, she was a brave and gallant woman, a great woman. It would mean so much to her uneasy spirit if you could recall what really happened to her son."

"I don't understand," Anna blurted suddenly. But something familiar was nagging at her.

"Her spirit has searched everywhere among the dead

and cannot find him. He was with *you* that night. You took him through the tunnel and tried to escape with him. Hanna . . . Anna . . . can you tell us what happened to him?"

"Why are you doing this to me?" Anna screamed in a sudden fury. "Go away, both of you. Leave me alone!"

"We are so sorry," whispered Mrs. Terwilliger, stepping backward through the wall.

"Wait! Wait!" Anna cried, frantically wheeling her chair out into the little corridor, down to the manager's office, and into the sun-filled lobby. "Wait!" she called again. Where were they?

Anna rushed out to the porch. She saw something far ahead, down the slope of the lawn. Something shimmering. Was it only a trick of the light?

The shimmering was moving farther away. Soon it was lost from sight among the bushes below.

Heaving herself out of the wheelchair, Anna sank down at the top of the stairs. Then she pushed herself from step to step, pulling the chair with her and trying, at the same time, to keep it from pulling away from her, toppling and crashing to the ground. It was hard, arm-wrenching work, but she managed. Once she climbed back into the chair, there was a wild chase down the slope, zigzagging and using the hand brake to keep from going too fast. But instead of slowing down, the chair became unbalanced. It lurched and overturned, falling on top of her as she rolled. And then it bounced away and was gone into the bushes.

Anna had fallen on soft, wet earth. Luckily, the chair had done little more than bruise her back. Letting herself roll the rest of the way to the bottom, she came to the little cemetery. The storm the night before had knocked down leaves and scattered small branches all over. A cool-blowing wind swirled everything about as if summer had already ended.

For as long as she'd lived with the Posts, Anna had dreaded cemeteries. It wasn't that she was more frightened of death than anyone else. It was as if places like this seemed to remind her of something gone horribly wrong, something that had been her fault. But the Terwilligers' disappearance had left her with a growing feeling of emptiness and sorrow. Then, squinting in the morning sunlight, she found their tombstones.

"I'm sorry!" she called to them. "I'm so sorry. Please forgive me for driving you away. But sometimes I get into a panic and . . . if you could just talk to me some more . . ."

Her voice drifted away. Nothing but the wind replied.

Then Anna saw the other grave, read the stone, and felt the hair rise on the back of her neck.

"Was this for me?" she gasped aloud. "Am I supposed to be buried here?" She read the stone again, more carefully:

THIS GRAVE LIES WAITING FOR OUR DEARLY BELOVED CHILD, HANNA.

Waiting!

Waiting for my body!

The moaning wind behind her carried a voice from a grave. "No, child, no. Waiting for you to come back through it."

Come back through it? What did that mean? A vague memory seemed to come back to Anna. Or was it simply her imagination going wild?

Whatever it was, Anna couldn't believe the insanity of what she did next. Her mind was telling her one thing—Get away from here!—but her hands, with a stick in them now, kept poking into the rain-softened earth of the grave of a missing child!

About a foot and a half down, the stick clattered against something hard.

"Oh, my God, what am I doing *now?*" Anna asked herself while clearing the earth away. "I've gone completely nuts! I'm trying to open the lid of a coffin!"

But if this was a coffin, it had an awfully strange shape— round and about two and a half feet across. It looked more like a barrel top with a kind of knob sticking up from the middle of it. Anna thought she'd need all of her strength to pull on the knob, but it broke right off in her hand, taking a chunk of the lid with it. Loose clods of earth fell inside.

But Anna had no desire to look inside, not until she poked a stick in and found the hole was empty. She was able to make absolutely sure because, thankfully, it wasn't very deep. If she were standing at the bottom of the hole, the opening would be just above her chin.

Gazing down into it now, Anna noticed that there was another hole off to one side of it, a hole that snaked away into blackness. Hold on a second, she told herself, was it the tunnel? The one she'd imagined the night before? If so, maybe it led to the hotel. Pulling up the rest of the top, Anna leaned over the hole, waiting for some idea to come to her about what to do next.

The tunnel seemed to be waiting, too. She stuck her head into the hole. She felt around. And she thought about doing something that was really, really stupid.

If I get down into it, how will I get *out*?

Anna heaved a sigh. End of experiment. She'd have to crawl up the slope as best she could, and get her parents to come down for the chair. She started to turn away.

Then she felt something—the tiniest little hand— tugging at her foot. And she thought she heard a sob.

Anna looked around quickly. Nothing.

This was weird. She had to get out of here! Her left foot gave her just the slightest bit of traction, but for the most part she had to push down and backward with her arms.

But the farther away she moved, the more ashamed she got. And again she couldn't tell why.

Okay! Okay. I'm going in!

Before she could change her mind, Anna went headfirst into the narrow hole.

But her dragging feet pulled much of the scooped-out dirt back in behind her. The tumbling earth worried her. Looking back, she saw that the wind was pasting twigs and leaves over what was left of the opening. In a few seconds she wouldn't be able to see the sky.

"Well, forget *this*!" she told herself.

But when she tried to wriggle around in the small space, she knocked against one of the boards that were holding up the sides of the crawl tunnel. The rotting wood gave way with a crunch, and more earth and small stones fell in on top of her. With desperately clawing fingers, she dragged herself through it.

Face down on the earth, and panting, Anna tried to peer into the darkness in front of her. But this was blacker than the blackness of a room at night with the lights out. Or like having pulled the covers over your head. But then you always knew you could escape the moment you wanted to, while this . . .

This was like being dead.

Anna shut her eyes as she dragged herself along. That way she could pretend to herself that she was making her own darkness. She played mind games to keep from noticing how her arms ached. She tried singing when she stopped to rest. But that was hard to do while panting and lying on her belly like a snake.

Most of all, she tried not to think of what would happen if she ever got to the other end of this endless tunnel only to find that it, too, was blocked.

Anna drove herself harder and harder, her arms aching, her fingers bleeding. Suddenly, she panicked. Her throat choked up. She felt smothered. If she didn't cry out, she wouldn't be able to breathe! She burst out screaming, screaming for help.

From a distance she heard a faint voice, calling, "Hanna! Hanna! Where is you?"

"I'm in here," she called back. "In the tunnel."

"Well, come on out of there, girl."

"But I'm scared."

"Ain't nothin' to be scared 'bout. You went in there all by your own self, didn't you?"

"Y-yes." She sniffled.

"Then just come on back."

"I'm a-tryin' to. But my legs don't want to help me, Rosalie. Some dirt fell in on them and they don't want to move."

"Wait there and I'll come in after you."

"No." She sniffled, feeling safer already. "I'm a-gonna try again."

She began to move, her knees curling under her.

"I'm all right now," she called.

And she began to crawl toward the voice.

The chief of police feared the worst when Mrs. Post's foot sank in among the leaves that had blown over little Hanna Terwilliger's unfilled grave. When he looked inside and found no freshly murdered child, he was glad to pull away from it and search someplace else. But Anna's father couldn't help thinking about Anna mentioning a tunnel the night before when he'd asked her to describe something about this place that they hadn't just seen together. Lying flat on his stomach, he studied this empty hole more closely.

"Look at that side!" he told himself. "The earth's softer over there, less packed than anyplace else. It could have fallen in today!"

Scrambling quickly to his feet, he told the police chief he wanted them to dig right away. The chief felt badly for the parents, but he thought it was all too farfetched.

"I'd like to do what you ask just to ease your mind," he told Mr. Post. "But the law is the law." He wondered if he should call the district attorney to ask if he had to get a court order to dig out any part of the grave.

Allan Post wouldn't wait. "I'm telling you, my

daughter could be down there in a tunnel!" he shouted. "And if it's caved in on her, then she's suffocating!"

He dashed back up the slope to the toolshed that stood behind the back of the former hotel. It was locked, but he ran straight at the rickety old door, slamming his body into it, and crashed it open. There was a shovel inside. Grabbing it, he rushed back down the slope to the open grave.

"You want to arrest me?" he yelled, waving the shovel at the officers. "Go ahead! But not till I'm finished!"

Jumping into the hole, he frantically began to clear away the soft earth. Fifteen minutes later, he discovered the tunnel. Getting down on his knees, he disappeared from sight, shouting for his daughter.

Had he been about four hours earlier, he might have had a chance to overtake her. But now he was over one hundred and forty years too late.

FIVE

"You see the light of my lantern yet?" called the voice at the far end of the tunnel.

Hanna Terwilliger wiped her tearful eyes with the back of her hand and blinked into the darkness. "No'm. I wish I could. But I cain't!"

"That's all right. Just keep comin' to my voice and you be all right. I'm waitin' for you right here, and I won't go away. But you might wish I had once I gets my hands on you."

"I done got turned around, Rosalie."

"*What?* You mean you was gonna crawl all that way to the graveyard when the tunnel ain't even finished yet down that end?"

"Well, they's a *little* hole there, Rosalie. I was gonna wiggle out through it and then hurry up to the house while Papa's still on the porch a-smokin' his cigar and surprise him and tell him his tunnel worked!"

"Is that right?"

"Yes, it is. But then I stopped to rest for a minute and . . . and then I fell asleep."

"You *fell asleep* in there?"

"Rosalie, it's powerful *dark!*"

"But takin' a nap in a *tunnel?*"

51

"Well . . . well, I don't know. I think so. I had such strange dreams, too. I had a different mama and papa. And I was a lot bigger, too. But I couldn't walk or crawl 'cause somethin' had happened to me, and nobody had any idea what it was."

"Well, I think you have a pretty good idea what's gonna happen to you now. Tell me somethin'. Was you gonna tell your pappy about the crawl tunnel in front of all those guests on the porch?"

"I . . . I guess so."

"And supposin' they asked you what the tunnel was for? You were gonna tell them that, too?"

"No . . . I guess not."

"You guess?"

"Rosalie, I wouldn't!"

"I don't understand you. Here you are, goin' on nine years old. But you done forgot everythin' we told you 'bout what could happen if somebody found out about this here hidin' place and the tunnel, and tells the law."

"But, Rosalie, I'll never do it again. Cross my heart and hope to die!"

"Don't be so fast to talk 'bout dyin'. You never seen any of that yet. All right now, I make you out in there. See my lantern?"

"Yes'm."

"But now you stoppin'. What you holdin' back for? Come on, I won't spank you this time."

As Hanna neared the tunnel's mouth, the lantern disappeared for a moment. Then large hands pulled her into the room.

Once the tiny room had been part of the hotel's basement, but now it was sealed off so that no one could find it. A ladder led up to a trapdoor in the ceiling, but otherwise the place was like a dungeon. There were no windows. Air came in through a pipe in the ceiling. And unless the trapdoor was open, there was no light. A few beds and a table with chairs were the only furniture.

After setting the girl down, Rosalie Sims picked up the lantern and inspected her. "My, you are dirty!"

"You gonna tell on me?"

"You don't think I should?"

"Y-e-s. But I surely wish you wouldn't."

"I'm too happy to tell on anybody right now. I'm just tryin' to keep from gettin' any happier in case somethin' goes wrong like it most always does if you don't look out. But if the Lord stay with me one more time, I'm gonna see my Li'l Rafe at last. First time, I reckon, in four years. And I don't have to sneak him out of Kentucky like me and your mama been doin' with all the others. The money to buy him's done been paid already, and I'm gonna get a paper from a lawyer that say he's set free. Ain't nobody gonna put their hands on him when I'm holdin' that bill of sale. I'm gonna take him with me for everyone to see right through the middle of that cracker-barrel town—a free woman with a free son! Away from that farm and out of slavery, and he ain't never goin' back."

"Am I goin' to the lawyer with you?"

"No. You and your mama are goin' just as far as the weddin' at your aunt's. Now you used up enough of my time lookin' for you. Go on up to your room and get yourself washed and dressed. We be leavin' presently."

Hanna put one foot on the ladder and turned around. "But I don't want to go to the weddin'."

"No? How come?"

"Because Papa won't go."

"Man has his reasons. He got this hotel to run."

"He could leave it. Mama says we been a-feedin' the schoolteacher all summer since the school closed down. She says he ought to be willin' to do some kind of work to pay us back."

"When I gets the time, he's gonna be teachin' me to read and write. Then I'll pay the hotel back for the hams and corn dodgers we been sendin' over to his cabin. 'Sides, he's gonna be teachin' my Rafe. And if your daddy don't want to go to that weddin', he's got good reasons. Your mama's family, they don't like him. You know that."

"'Cause they say he's a Yankee?"

"If he was a Yankee what didn't mind them keepin' my people in chains, they'd like him some better, I'll tell you that much."

"Papa says I should call you Mrs. Sims, like he does. To show you respect."

"Why? You don't respect me when you call me Rosalie."

"Yes, I do. Papa says you're famous all over the slave country, only people don't know what your real name is."

"My real name got took from me a long time before I was born."

"Mama says Sims was probably the name of your first master."

"Don't call any man master. That word should belong to no one but the good Lord. 'Specially the man what's got my son now. I heard tell that he don't hardly feed my boy most days."

Rosalie looked as if she was about to have one of her spells of bad temper. They only happened to her when she thought about the seven-year-old son she had been trying for so long to find and set free. Hanna went on anyway. "But Daddy says it's powerful dangerous for you to go. People there are startin' to 'spect who you are. He says it don't matter that we're fixin' to buy Li'l Rafe free—"

"I'm the one what's buyin' my child free! Don't you forget that. I did it with my own earnin's as a free woman. Your folks bought me free, and I bless 'em for that. But the rest I done for myself."

"I know that. But he says it might be a trap to catch

you. He says they might know already how you been fetchin' runaway slaves out of there. That's why Mama thinks she ought to go to the lawyer 'stead of you. Only she's afraid you'd get some angry if she told you."

"'Deed I would get angry! *You* are her child; Li'l Rafe is *mine*! Besides, your mama and I done all the same things together."

"Yes, but Mama says they'd a-hang you, sure enough, Rosalie. If they caught her, why she's a lady of the Old South. They'd just a-blame Papa for makin' her into a 'bolitionist and get her to promise not to do it anymore."

Rosalie shook her head and sighed. "She done said a thing like that? I swear, sometimes that woman's a bigger worry to me than you are. 'Course, she was only tryin' to make your pappy feel better. But they find out about what your mammy's been doin' this last year or so, they gonna change their minds real quick. So don't you blab nothin' 'bout it at the weddin'. You mindin' me?"

"Yes'm."

"I mean it now." Rosalie stared at Hanna. "You do a lot of listenin' in, huh? 'Specially when you suppose to be sleepin'. Put your ear to the door when your folks is a-talkin' in bed?"

Hanna felt her cheeks burn under Rosalie's stern gaze. "Reckon I'll go upstairs now," she said in a tiny voice.

"And I reckon maybe all that sneakin' around is why you can't keep your eyes open in tunnels. Think that's what it is?"

"But I'm glad I had that dream, Rosalie. 'Cause it's important!"

"I 'spect you'll tell me more 'bout it on the way to Kentucky."

"I dunno. I'm beginnin' to forget it already. And I don't want to."

"Why? What was so important 'bout it?"

"There's somethin' I got to do."

"What is it?"

"I don't know."

Years of hard work had roughened Rosalie's fingers, yet they touched Hanna's face gently. "Sweetness, you been dreamin' your fears. Now you got a good heart. But don't you go puttin' too much heaviness into it yet. You got some growin' up to do 'fore then. Go on up the ladder. Mind you, pull that rug over it again, so nobody can see the hatch. Then hurry up and wash and dress. Your mama laid your clothes out on the bed. Still a ways to go 'fore we get to the ferry, then across the Ohio. And there some plenty drivin' after that. We don't want to be on the road after dark."

SIX

Hanna had come out of the tunnel barefoot, wearing a torn shirt, pants, and suspenders. It was how she liked to dress when she could get away with it. This was a good deal of the time, what with the secret digging in the basement and many of the guests upstairs calling her country tomboy ways "charming."

"Oh yes, it's certainly charming, all right," her mother would huff. "As long as it's not *their* daughter."

Now, though, she was all dressed up in new white shoes, a petticoat under a green summer dress, and a matching bonnet. It made her feel as uncomfortable as when she had to sit through church and Sunday school in one long sitting. Still with a bit of prodding from Rosalie, she was perched like a little lady on the driver's seat of the buggy when her mother came down the steps with her father.

Just the sight of them made Hanna's heart jump, though she didn't know why. She felt as if she hadn't seen them for years and years, although the truth was, they had taken breakfast together just after daybreak, before the guests were up.

When the guests came down, Mama would talk to

the ladies about this and that, children mostly. Papa and the men would talk about the new railroads going inland away from the rivers, and how they might be good for the farmers and bad for the boat owners. And they would discuss the war some of them had fought against Mexico, where Papa had been a hero.

The one thing Papa never spoke to them about, though, was slavery. Nearly half of the guests who came to the hotel had slaves of their own back home south of the Ohio River.

"Men can have different opinions on almost everything else and still be friendly," Mama had explained to Hanna once. "But when it comes to slavery being right or wrong, they want to kill each other."

Hanna knew how hard it was for her papa not to really say what was on his mind in his own place of business. She'd hear him complaining to her mother, when he'd push away his food untouched. It gave him great pains in the stomach sometimes to listen and nod his head while these men talked to one another over their cigars and bourbon about the good deals they had made buying or selling this slave or that.

Mama hated it even more. It made her furious to hear one plantation owner's wife telling another about how she had to horsewhip some slave girl for doing a terrible, careless thing like dropping silverware on the floor in the middle of dinner.

But Mama had long ago learned not to show those feelings. She just had to wait and bide her time until she could do something about them. And whenever she was just dying to up and give one of those women a large piece of her mind, she would think of the one thing that calmed her right down. If it hadn't been for these "upstanding guests" sitting in her parlor and playing croquet on her lawn, the county sheriff would have come nosing around a long time ago to look for runaways from across the river in slave country.

Coming down the steps together, Hanna's parents were doing something Hanna had never seen before—not in front of other people. They were holding hands, like two children.

"What is it?" Rosalie, who was sitting beside her, asked, noticing the amazed look on the girl's face.

"Look how young Mama is! I never knowed she was so young 'fore. And Papa, he didn't lose his arm!"

"Do you feel all right?" Rosalie looked at her strangely.

"That was in my dream, Rosalie. Papa had only one arm, and his hair was white, and you could see right through both of—"

"I don't think this is a good time to talk 'bout no kind of foretellin' dream," Rosalie said hastily. "Your father looks worried enough without that. Maybe when we get back, I'll take you to the Conjure Woman to make some head or tail of it."

"Is this really Hanna?" Amos Terwilliger said, coming up to her. His serious expression changed into a wonderfully beaming smile. "You look like Cinderella on her way to the ball."

"It's gonna be a weddin', Papa."

"Oh, I imagine there'll be a ball afterward."

"I think she'll be sleeping afterward," said her mother. "We'll want to leave real early to make the ferry home, just as soon as Rosalie comes back with Little Rafe from the lawyer's in Elizabethtown."

The serious look returned to Papa's face as he turned to Rosalie. "I think you already know how I feel about you going along with them, Mrs. Sims."

"Yes, I know. And I thank you for worryin' 'bout me. But I've been over many a-time for other people's children. This time it's for mine."

"Things have changed down there," Papa said. "There's a lot of anger and violence in the air. The word I'm getting almost every day is that the South is almost ready to go to war unless a lot more is done by the government to stop their slaves from running off."

"This here's got nothin' to do with the Underground Railroad. The lawyer done took the money already and passed it along to the man what has my little boy, didn't he?"

"So he wrote to me. But if anyone even suspects that you're Mother Freedom, they may be using this to get you over there. The price on your head has been doubled again, I'm afraid."

Rosalie sat up straighter. "Goes to show what freedom does for a woman, don't it? Now I'm more valuable to 'em than when I was somebody's slave."

"I wouldn't joke about this," Papa said.

"All the more reason I should go across alone and not with Dora and the child."

"That's out of the question," declared Mrs. Terwilliger firmly. "No Negro woman is going to drive a buggy through slave country by herself and not get stopped. And if she falls into the wrong hands, it won't matter that she's carrying papers to show she's been set free. There are those who don't care about papers. They'll burn the papers and accuse her of stealing the buggy. Then they'll take it for themselves and sell *her* off, as well. I've seen it happen before."

Rosalie turned in her seat. "Then Dora, at least don't take the child."

"That's where you and I agree very strongly," declared Hanna's father.

"Now listen here, both of you," said Mrs. Terwilliger, growing so angry that her southern accent began to show. "It was my aunt who taught me about books and poetry and to think for myself about the meaning of things. She's eighty-six years old, and her health is failing. She wants to bring this family together, and to see her niece one last time before she dies."

Amos Terwilliger's dark brown mustache twitched. "I'm talking about safety," he said softly. "You're being stubborn, dearest."

"Yes, I am. And I can tell you this, Amos." Making sure that no one could see her from the porch, Mama brought out a pistol from the folds of her clothing. "I'm as good a shot as you are. Nothing on God's earth is going to happen to my Hanna while I'm alive to stop it. Now help me to my seat like a gentleman, or I'll do it myself."

Hanna had watched her mother climb alone into the buggy a thousand times. Then Hanna realized that Mama wanted to feel Papa's strong arms holding her one more time. And she saw in her mother's eyes just a little touch of the worry that she was hiding.

Dora Terwilliger took up the reins and bent over to kiss her husband. "I love you, darling, for being so concerned. But you're going to be so busy with your guests and with widening that tunnel, we'll be back with Little Rafe before you notice it." Then she shook the reins. Johnny Appleseed didn't move.

"I do believe he knows he's goin' to the ferry," said Rosalie. "This is one horse that do hate crossin' over that river into slavery land."

Hanna heard her mutter under her breath, "And, the Lord help me, so do I."

SEVEN

It was a twelve-mile ride to the river. The closer to the ferry Johnny Appleseed pulled the buggy, the slower he went.

Getting him off the dock and onto the boat was even more of a chore. He'd done it often enough before, but each time he seemed to like it less. Now he plain balked, even with Hanna carefully stepping backward onto the plank deck, pulling pieces of maple sugar off a string to hold in front of him.

Mama suggested that his reluctance might be because of the ferryman. Johnny Appleseed was a "sensitive creature," and the man always had a nasty look under that dirty red bandanna that he wore pirate style around his balding head. The horse was taking it personally.

But Hanna could tell that Rosalie had another opinion. Beneath the open seat of the buggy on which the three of them sat was a compartment with a piece of leather upholstery draped over it. Now it held a bale of hay, but at other times a slave with a terrible backache would be tightly squeezed inside of it. Horses needed to know that their driver felt confident, and a good horse could tell when its mistress was nervous. Johnny Appleseed had sensed a lot of fear in his time.

Rosalie was playing the part of a maid of all work. Hopping out of her seat, she gave Johnny Appleseed a stern slap, and dragged him on board. Then she put on a feed bag filled with oats over his muzzle, and stayed with him until he was settled.

The ferryman merely grunted at her as he poled away from the dock, and called her a name under his breath.

"That's enough!" Dora Terwilliger snapped at him.

"You don't like how I talk, you kin get off my boat, how's that?" he hurled back at her.

"Ignorant person," she huffed to herself and fell silent.

But Rosalie merely folded her arms after she got back onto her seat. "Man better watch out, 'cause I know what's under that bandanna he's got on."

"What's that?" Hanna asked.

"Kinky hair. Less he done shaved *all* of it off."

The wide river, glittering in the sun, was very busy. Several flatboats with men at the poles went by, heading west for the Mississippi. They were loaded with foodstuffs to be taken down South as far as New Orleans a thousand miles away. *The Pride of Dixie*, a steamboat with a paddle in the stern, was coming the other way. But today it probably wouldn't be pulling into shore at the nearby landing. The

Terwilligers weren't expecting any hotel guests to arrive or leave.

But Rosalie and Mama had their eyes on the long rowboats in the center of the river. They were stationed about a quarter mile apart, each of them filled with men whose rifle barrels glinted in the sun.

Their long Kentucky rifles, though old, were the cleanest thing about these men. They were unshaved and ragged, with torn shirts and jackets, and wore floppy, wide-brimmed hats to shield them from the sun. They passed jugs around as they sat carefully watching anybody who passed in any direction. They were especially interested in the ferry. It was the only boat that was *crossing* the river.

At a signal from their leader, one of men raised his gun and fired a shot that went directly over the ferry. The ferryman stopped poling.

Rosalie hopped out of her seat once again to calm the horse. That gave her the chance, Hanna noticed, to keep the men rowing toward them from getting a good look at her. Meanwhile, she pulled the kerchief she'd been wearing over her head even farther across the sides of her face.

The ferryman was cussing, but not loud enough for his words to travel over water. "Blast their eyes! Why're they doin' that? It's enough they shoot to stop boats a-comin' the other way. But sure as shootin' ain't no runaway slaves a-sneakin' *back*!

"Now gentlemen, listen here," he called out as the other boat drew near. "I shore would appreciate it if you'd just yell or hold up a hand if you want me to pull to. That'll be just fine and I'll know what you mean. Now what do you say to that?"

From the moment the men came near, Hanna had felt Mama's hand tighten in her own. She followed her mother's example, sitting up straight and looking patiently past the longboat at nothing in particular.

But the men weren't showing much interest in either of them, or in the ferryman either. They were staring at Rosalie, who somehow seemed to have grown much smaller. It was almost as if she were disappearing inside her long, loose muslin dress.

"Someone fetch me them reward posters," commanded the leader of the group.

One of the men handed him a small packet. Unwrapping the posters, the leader flipped through several of them, staring at the drawings and then at Rosalie. He held one to the light.

"What's this here say 'bout age and height and weight and all that?" Climbing up on the ferry, he thrust the poster with its badly drawn picture of Rosalie in Mama's face.

Hanna looked on as Mama read—and lied—about the description it gave of Mother Freedom.

"'Age,'" said Mama, "'between fifty and fifty-five.

Height five foot five to five foot seven. Weight approximately two hundred pounds.'"

"Hold on." The leader stared closely at Rosalie, who was strong but skinny. "This cain't be her then."

"That's true," said Mama, handing back the poster.

"But you angry with me. What's the matter? You don't like what we'uns are a-doin'?"

"That's no concern of mine." Mama's eyes flared. "But firing a gun in our direction and scaring a child half to death—"

"It didn't scare me, Mama," Hanna interrupted suddenly. "Don't be mad at them."

The bounty hunter swept off his hat and bowed. "Thank you, little missy."

"Welcome," Hanna replied as if she hadn't noticed the man's false politeness.

Now he was studying Mama up and down. "What's your reason for goin' to Kentucky?"

"To attend my cousin's wedding."

"That right?"

"Yes, it is," said Mama. And Hanna heard her mother's southern accent grow thicker.

"You don't sound like a Kentucky woman, though."

"Well, I am. But my family came from Virginia, and I was raised by an aunt to sound that way. I'm sorry if it offends you."

"No, don't offend me none. I'm from there myself.

But I just wonder if maybe you ain't a-readin' this to me just right."

"Why would I lie to you?"

"Oh, I cain't say why. But my experience is that fine folks lie to poor folks all the time."

He turned to the ferryman. "You cain't run a business and not read, right?"

"Some do. But I kin read pretty powerful good."

"Read me what it says here."

The ferryman had exaggerated his ability. While he was squinting in the sunlight over the page, Hanna suddenly stood up in her seat as if she was onstage.

"We are, too, from Kentucky!" she exclaimed, as if somebody had denied it. "And I'll prove it, right now."

Then she burst into reciting:

"Never saw me Old Virginia,
Where my grandpap he was born.
He set out one day for the Promised Land
A-leavin' with the dawn.

"Through the Cumberland Gap
On the Wilderness Trail
To the blue hills of Kaintuck,
My grandpap he come a-ridin' in
On hope and tech of luck.
He built a lean-to 'gainst the wind,

Put his family 'round the fire;
But the chill stayed there
Till he skinned two bear
And the wintertime grew tired."

"By jings, boys!" exclaimed one of the men. "Are you all a-listenin' to this?"

"When the spring leaves come
And the berries growed,
The trees he started clearin'.
But a tomahawk brought the good man down
When Grandma's time was a-nearin'."

"Ain't that how it was!" declared another man. "That were exactly how it was!"

"But she built her a cabin just before
My pappy was born on an earthen floor
With leather hinges on the door,
And she raised him up God-fearin'."

Hanna had noticed Rosalie stealing a glance at the leader and the ferryman. It made her forget what she'd said last. Meanwhile, the others were urging her on. She took just long enough to be sure that the leader was looking away from the poster now, his eyes as damp as any of theirs. Sending him a quick little smile, she continued:

"And she raised him up God-fearin'
With buckskin britches and birch bark shoes
And a shirt all torn and tattered.
Yet till she up and died one night
Warn't none of it that mattered."

A loud sob came like a thunderclap from the longboat. One of the men stood up and declared, "This here child is like an angel."

Hanna turned, and her large, sad brown eyes looked straight at him.

"Then he married up with my sweet ma
Whilst both were still a-growin',
And I was born on a corn shuck bed
While the storm winds were a-blowin'."

"Lordy, but it's a hard life, a hard life!" said one of the men, sighing.

She turned her eyes on that one now.

"And my mammy took right care of me
Till the day she lay a-dyin'.
Then my pa, he sent me far away,
Yet for his good soul I daily pray
Like a blessin' I'm bestowin'."

"Preacher don't say it better'n her!"

"Cain't none of you shut up? Let this girl a-finish!"

> "Oh, this land is rich, but the farmer's poor,
> Still of one thing I am certain:
> Till I set foot on Kaintucky's shore,
> My heart will stay a-hurtin'."

Hanna finished, and whether silently or loudly, they were all crying now.

"Little missy," said one man, "I surely thank you. That were some beautiful. Ma'am you should be proud of her."

"Yes, I am. And surprised, too."

"Well, come on, boys. Let's go," said the leader.

They waited in silence until the longboat was gone. "Trash!" said Rosalie, grunting, and she spat into the water. "Nothin' but trash."

But Mama shook her head, sighing deeply. "Yes, *now* they are. And it's such a shame! Those are the very people who should be fighting *against* slavery, not *for* it. If it weren't for the rich people bringing more and more slaves into Kentucky to do all their farming for next to nothing, these men wouldn't be so ragged. They'd still have their homes, no matter how humble. And more important, still have enough pride in themselves."

Mama started another deep sigh; but before it was completed, a large grin began to spread across her face. Lifting Hanna's bonnet, she rumpled her daughter's hair.

"Why, you little actress, you! The way you turned down the corners of your mouth and made those sad, soulful eyes at them. I can't believe that you remembered all the words to that terrible poem. Who taught it to you?"

"It was that senator, Mama, who visited last year. But I disremembered some of it. Had to make some up."

"Why do you say words like *disremember?*" Mama chided her gently. "You don't have to talk like that now."

"She wants to be like the other children at school," Rosalie explained. "Tell you all what bothers me," she went on. "I didn't care what she *disremembered*. I cared what she *remembered*. That was goin' on so long, I'd just 'bout made up my mind to jump in that longboat and say, 'Whatever it is, I confess. Take me to jail or shoot me. Only just do it now!'"

They all had a good laugh over that. But their happiness was short-lived. The vigilante leader had gone off without the poster. And the ferryman had finally been able to make out what it said.

"You done lied 'bout the description," he told Mama darkly. Then he settled his eyes on Mother Freedom.

Rosalie walked boldly up to him. "Found out 'bout

you last time over. You grandmother was a slave. I even know the plantation she was on. White folks in Kentucky gonna let you run this ferry back and forth if they find out who you is? Or maybe you thinkin' 'bout some reward. No black man gets a reward, no matter what he gets promised. And one thing more." Rosalie reached into her dress and brought out a gun. "See this revolver? Got six bullets in it. If I don't get to pump 'em all in you, they's others that will. We understand each other now?"

Their eyes went to war, until he looked away. He opened his mouth as if to answer, but he only spit in the water.

"I'll think on it," he growled at last. And nothing more was said until the ferry docked.

EIGHT

They had landed in a little hamlet far from the big riverfront towns. Johnny Appleseed was glad to get off the boat. He made good time trotting away from the landing and onto a dirt road lined with wild crab apple trees and broken-down shacks. Ragged white children played outside of them, while old people with dried-up faces sat in rickety chairs on sagging porches. The smoke from their corncob pipes curled up above the tiny plots of land that once were farms but now grew little more than weeds.

Rosalie looked at them carefully as they drove by. "I agree with some part of what you said 'fore, Dora. These folks aren't all the way free themselves yet. But some of it is just in their minds."

"What's in people's heads is important, Rosalie," Hanna said.

The two women smiled at Hanna, and her mother tickled her under the chin. "Like what, child?"

"Like dreams, Mama."

"She done had some sort of crazy dream."

"They come after Little Rafe, Mama. Back home. They had guns and torches, and I took him out through the tunnel. But . . . "

"But what, child?"

Hanna's trembling began with her shoulders and fingers. In a few seconds her entire body rattled out of control.

Mrs. Terwilliger was so alarmed that she yanked on the reins to halt the horse. "My dear, what's the matter? Let me touch your head. Are you having chills?"

"She got the fever?"

"No. She isn't hot. She's cold. Her hands are turning to ice! Oh, I don't like this at all. It's what happened with those men; I'm sure of it."

"No, M-m-mama."

"Yes," insisted her mother, who suddenly turned comforting. "You're just beginning to feel the strain of it. That's natural, child. That sometimes happens after it's all over and you feel you can let go." She wrapped her daughter in her arms. "Why, your teeth are chattering, poor dear. Rosalie, would you please fetch something warm from the big bag? I put her favorite blanket in there."

Suddenly, Hanna peered at her mother with glowing eyes. "P-p-please, don't be angry if . . . if I ask you this, Mama. If I had another mama and papa somewhere's else, w-would they be s-something worried and a-lookin' for me now? I r-really think I hear s-somebody a-c-callin' my name. Only it's A-a-anna."

"She's delirious," gasped Dora. "Oh, my heavens! Could it be the milk sick?"

"Give a look at her tongue," said Rosalie, standing on her seat, hurriedly untying the bag. "Her tongue be all covered with white if she has the milk sick."

"But already?"

"Oh, yeah."

"Open your mouth, sweet lamb, if you can hear me, and show me your tongue."

Hanna tried, but her chattering teeth made her bite it instead. Mrs. Terwilliger forced the child's jaws open. "No, it's red."

"All right then. That dream is what it is. She had it in the tunnel."

"In the tunnel!"

"Rosalie, you b-broke your promise!" Hanna cried.

"I know, but your sleepin' in the tunnel has somethin' to do with it. And when we gets back, I'm gonna take you to the Conjure Woman and find out what it means."

"Rosalie, do you actually believe in that business?"

"Maybe yes, maybe no. But that woman be over a hundred years old and still runnin' like a clock! Don't you figure she knows *somethin'* 'bout gettin' through this here life that we don't?"

"I suppose."

"Me, too. Now why don't you keep that young'un warm in your arms and let me sit there behind old Johnny. Look better to the white folks if I'm the one drivin' *you*."

They had meant to make a little stop along the way at the home of a brave family of Quakers. The hayloft in their barn was the last secret hiding place in slave country before runaways fled across the Ohio.

But Dora and Rosalie thought better of doing it now. The quicker they got to Aunt Ida's, the faster Hanna would lie quietly in the bed in her mother's old room. Besides, things seemed to be going wrong from the start on this trip, and they wanted to get it over with.

Despite her chills and the jogging of the buggy, Hanna fell asleep. She saw a man whose face was hard to make out. He was on his hands and knees, crawling through the tunnel. But the tunnel was blocked by fallen earth, and he couldn't get into the secret room. He stopped and turned around—and seemed to be crying.

Then he was standing in the windy graveyard, holding a woman who sobbed desperately, "Then she might still be alive! But where has she gone?"

Hanna thought they meant her. She called to them. "Here I am! Right here!"

But they didn't hear her, couldn't see her. They turned away, walking slowly up the slope to the hotel. Hanna remained behind in the graveyard, because she realized that there were three more headstones there than she remembered. Going closer, she saw that one of them had Papa's name on it. The one next to it said that Mama was buried there. And tucked away just at the mouth of the tunnel, there was one that had *her* name on it. "Born 1841" it said. "Died 1850. By slave hunters somewhere cruelly murdered."

She screamed aloud, and immediately woke up. Mama was kissing her face. "My little darling. My little precious. Your father was right. I was so stubborn. I should never have brought you here with us."

"What's done is done," said Rosalie, shaking the reins to keep Johnny Appleseed from dipping his head to catch some blades of grass. "Giddap, horse. You'll be eatin' fine presently."

It was nightfall before they passed between twin hills, climbed for a bit, and rode down into Fairweather Valley. Moonlight welcomed them past fields of corn and long corrals and pastures for fine horses. Exhausted as he was, Johnny Appleseed hurried through the gate. He smelled great stacks of freshly mowed hay, and longed for his feed bag to be filled again with oats. There might be more maple sugar treats—and certainly a bucketful of water—waiting for him in the stall.

For several hours, Hanna had been sleeping without bad dreams in her mother's arms. She woke to hear Rosalie say, "I'm thinkin' I don't want to stay the night. I want to get there fast and see what's up."

"But the horse will be much too tired."

"I don't want him. I need another horse. Don't want the buggy either. You said yourself, anybody see a colored woman in a fancy buggy like this, they gonna stop me and say I stole it. And there no way you kin go with me tonight, 'specially with the baby sick."

"Rosalie, I'm not a baby."

"Just a word, sweetness! But no, you ain't. You sure proved that on the ferry. Let me finish talkin' to your mama. Dora, I want to go there in my own way, with a buckboard totin' some potato sacks or somethin' like that, to look like I'm just haulin' a delivery. Kin you arrange that?"

"Just take it, and I'll tell my aunt—if she even asks—that you went to see relatives. But I hate to see you go by yourself."

"Got to. The closer I get to this, the more of a feelin' I have that your husband wasn't wrong 'bout there bein' trouble waitin' for me. If there's some reason I have to steal my boy away 'stead of payin' for him, I'm gonna do it. And I don't want to lead 'em here. I'll go straight for the Quakers. When you finished with the weddin', go back to Indiana without me, so there's no problem on the ferry. I'll stay low, and when the search dies down a li'l, I'll find some other way to get me and Li'l Rafe over."

"How? No. We're in this together, Rosalie. Even if everything goes smoothly, the quicker you're back on the other side, the better. Regardless of what happens, come back here. I'll be ready at any time."

"Listen to me. It's freein' my son we're a-talkin' 'bout

now. It might be I'll have to shoot somebody. Still want me to come here?"

"Yes." There was a long silence and Mama sighed. "Might be I'll have to do the same."

"Get on, horse!" Rosalie shook the reins. Johnny Appleseed was very unhappy about going past the stables. But after a couple of snorts and head shakes, he moved on and turned up the circular path to the house.

It was a big place that Mama's father, Adam Fairweather, had built to resemble General George Washington's home in Virginia. The old man had never forgotten the day he stood by the side of the road to cheer the general as he rode slowly north all by himself to be sworn in as president. When young Adam had called out, "My father was with you at Valley Forge," the general stopped to talk to him and learned the boy had become an orphan. Then, leaning down from his saddle, he had swept him up in one arm and given him a ride on his beautiful horse.

A slave had been waiting for hours at the door for the first sight of them. The moment they arrived, he rushed inside to tell Mistress Ida. Another slave came up to lead Johnny Appleseed off, but Mama shook her head.

"No, we'll do that ourselves, Isaiah," she said, stepping down quickly and taking the still groggy Hanna in her arms. "I'm truly glad to see you, but I cannot be against slavery and make use of it at the same time. This is Mrs. Sims. She's a free woman and she works for me. I've asked her to care for the horse. She will also need the use of a buckboard right away. So if you wouldn't mind telling the stable hand I said it was all right, I'd appreciate it. How is your wife?"

"Poorly, missus."

"I'm sorry. I'll go to see her as soon as I can."

"Yes, missus. She surely would like that."

Mama walked to the bottom of the stairs, and then paused. "Has my aunt said anything to you about the . . . uh . . . future?"

Isaiah looked puzzled.

"Never mind."

Just then Aunt Ida appeared. The slender, bespectacled old lady gave Hanna a start. There was something about her that reminded her so much of someone in her dream. . . .

"So this is Hanna!" In spite of her cane, the woman almost flew down the long flight of steps. "Dear me, what a beautiful girl you are! And so big. I want your arms around my neck this instant! And give me a kiss. Yes, that's it. Nine long years I've longed so to see you, but your grandfather . . . Well, but that's another story."

Aunt Ida stepped back and studied Hanna. "Child, why is your mother carrying you?"

"She isn't feeling well."

"Yes, I am, Mama; right as rain. Reckon you kin put me down right now."

"Why is she talking as if she's from the backwoods?

84

Don't you give young people an education over in Indiana?"

"Please, don't start with me, Aunt Ida. I just want to get her to bed quickly."

"Why? What's the matter with the child?" Aunt Ida was suddenly alarmed.

"She just . . . had an unpleasant time of it coming over on the ferry. I'll tell you about it later."

"Isaiah, why are you standing there? Are you going to let her lug that child up the stairs by herself?"

"I'm sorry, mistress, but she don't want me to do nothin'."

"Why in the world not?"

"Aunt Ida, you know perfectly well. And you made me a promise! Otherwise I wouldn't have come."

Dora started up the steps, with Ida right behind her. "And I kept it, too," the old lady said in a low voice. "I put it in my will just as I said I would. They are going to be set free when I'm gone. All of them. And with a few dollars, too."

"Then how is it Isaiah doesn't know anything about it?"

"Because . . . " Ida waited until they'd passed through the doorway to finish her sentence. "I don't see the sense of giving *anybody* a reason for sending up prayers every night for me to die quickly. Especially not when I've got so much catching up to do, getting to know my grandniece. Where are you taking her?"

"To my old room. I want her to stay with me tonight." Dora headed for the stairs.

"Then I'm coming, too. It's a big enough bed for the three of us, and there's a lot that I want to hear. In particular, I want to know what kind of trouble you're in."

"Why should I be in trouble?"

"You don't fool me, Dora. Not one little bit. You have never fooled me. You came back for some other purpose than to see a second cousin get married to a man you couldn't stand when he was chasing *you*. And I intend to have the truth."

Sagging under the weight of her daughter, Dora Terwilliger paused in the middle of the stairs to catch her breath. "Believe me," she panted, "it's nothing at all. We're just going to buy somebody's freedom."

"Why all this secrecy then with that woman of yours slipping off like that? And why was she standing on the other side of the horse as if she was hiding her face? You don't think I notice such things?"

"Oh, Aunt Ida, she was just shy, that's all."

"Shy! You expect me to believe that?"

"Won't you *please* leave well enough alone!" Mama hurried up to the landing. "If I told you any more you wouldn't like it."

"Oh, I'm all a-flutter from this climb. Slow down! And whatever it is, I knew perfectly well from the start that I didn't *intend* to like it."

"Well, was I wrong about her, Hanna?" Mama opened a door down the hall and dropped her burden like a stone on the huge, frilly bed. "Haven't I told you more than once that your aunt was a difficult person?"

Hanna held her peace while the two women stared at each other for a long moment. Then she watched them fall into each other's arms, kissing and crying.

Lying there teary-eyed herself, Hanna wondered about Rosalie. She thought about those five long years of searching for Little Rafe. Five years of taking every kind of chance, going through every kind of danger. What would it be like between the two of them when a mother and her son—one free and the other a slave—finally laid eyes on each other?

Hanna prayed that everything would go well, while she listened to her mother keep changing the subject until Aunt Ida gave up trying to learn anything more.

And later, when they were all chattering away, Hanna heard sounds through the open window—the whinny of a horse being led out into the darkness and the distant creak of a wagon.

NINE

Amanda was the name of the bride. She'd arrived the day before and was staying with her parents in another part of the Fairweather house. Hanna and Dora didn't get to meet them until the next morning, when there was too much excitement for anyone to sit still for breakfast.

The bride had discovered something horribly wrong with her wedding gown. Actually, it was nothing more than a few threads out of place. But that wasn't what really worried her. Nobody had heard from her husband-to-be in days. What if something was keeping him from getting here on time? Or worse still, what if he'd changed his mind and wasn't coming at all?

"Of course he'll be here!" cried Amanda's mama. "He is a man of his word and lucky to be getting you!" What bothered her was that the sky was clouding over and it looked as if there was going to be rain. She had so wanted the ceremony to be outside, under a huge sycamore tree, with the best voices among Aunt Ida's slaves singing spirituals. But if it even started to shower, everything would have to be moved inside the house. They would have to start rehearsing the wedding procession all over again. And that wasn't even half of what would have to be changed at the last minute!

At first Aunt Ida tried to be a voice for calmness, but then she threw up her hands. "What happened to the *joy* of this occasion? Where is the *happiness* here? If I have to listen to one more complaint or watch one more nit-picking worry being turned into the disaster of all time, then I am going to cancel having this wedding here! You can go and have it performed in a post office for all I care."

Amanda's father cast angry glances at his wife and daughter. Then he rushed over to beg Aunt Ida's pardon for all the inconvenience. Why, he couldn't begin to tell her what an honor it was that his only child was going to be married in Fairweather Hall. It was as if Aunt Ida was giving this marriage her special blessing!

"What he really means," Aunt Ida muttered to Hanna in private, "is that he wants to make sure I've remembered to put Amanda in my will. I'm telling you, darling, I'm getting sick and tired of how impatient everyone seems to be to have me die."

"Not me and Mama."

Aunt Ida squeezed Hanna's hand and sighed. "No, that I believe. There isn't a practical bone in your mother's body. Why, she could have had all this for herself if your grandfather hadn't cut her off because she married a Yankee abolitionist. She has spunk, your mama. Not entirely a lot of common sense, but spunk. By the way, where is she? I haven't seen her for hours."

Hanna didn't want to lie, so she tried to act as if she hadn't heard the question. Mama had been nervously hurrying back and forth to the stable since before the sun came up.

But Aunt Ida was too smart for her. "Has to do with that woman, hasn't it? She's afraid for her, isn't she? I don't understand why, if all there is to it is a purchase and sale of property."

"Li'l Rafe isn't property, Aunt Ida. He's a person."

The old lady looked closely at Hanna. "So you're one of them, are you? A fire-eyed abolitionist. Tell me something: Are you part of the conspiracy, too? You'd better answer me, child. I know something is going on. And if your mother has foolishly put you into danger, I want to try to protect *you*."

Hanna just shook her head. Aunt Ida threw up her hands in despair. "Oh, get on with you! Wait a minute. Come back. I want you to go and ask your mother to come here right away. When the wedding guests start arriving, we won't have time to talk in private. And there's something important I need to tell her."

Ducking under a fence post into the horse pasture, Hanna ran across it to the gate near the stables on the other side. Just as she was about to open it, Hanna heard galloping hoofbeats and saw her mother come rushing out of the stable in the hope that it was Rosalie. But it was a man on horseback, wearing a tall gray hat and a jacket with long coattails. Even before the horse came to a full stop, he leaped off in front of Mrs. Terwilliger, and took her by the hand.

"Dora! This may be my wedding day, but I hope you know I have never stopped loving you."

"Sir! Please control yourself. That is my daughter standing over there."

The man looked at Hanna over his shoulder but did not let go of the hand. "She's very beautiful, just like her mother. And I'm not ashamed of my feelings. They are honorable, and always were. If I did not regard your wishes as the most important thing in my life, I would have killed your future husband in a duel before he could take you away with him."

"I'd have hated you for that, Austin."

"I know. But still it was a mistake to let him live. I know what a terrible thing he has done to you."

Hanna's mother angrily yanked her hand away. "What are you talking about?"

"The man's opinions do not matter to me. He can be as much an enemy of our way of life as he likes, so long as *he* is the one who acts upon it. But when he stays home in the safety of Indiana and sends you to do his dirty work—"

Mama's slap across the man's face cracked like a whip and sent the hat flying from his head. "You will not speak of my husband that way! And certainly not in front of his own child."

He glared at her, but only for a moment. "I had

forgotten about your temper. But I thank you for reminding me." He bent down to pick up his hat and knocked sawdust off it. "I do so want to treasure all my memories of you."

"Oh, stop it, Austin. I have no patience with this. You are getting married today. Congratulations. Now go away."

"Why? So you can wait for Mother Freedom to arrive?"

Hanna's mother staggered back. "What are you talking about?"

"Surely you know that I'm in Congress now, Dora."

"What has that—?"

"I'm on the committee that deals with fugitive slaves. I've been helping to prepare the new law that will force the government to go after all the runaway slaves in the North and bring them back. But first I've had to gather facts, evidence of agitators coming down into my state. People like you, Dora, and that woman Rosalie Sims. You pretend to go on shopping trips to Louisville or to visit some old schoolgirl chum. And after the two of you leave, there's always another slave missing from someplace nearby. You smuggle them north in different ways, I'm sure. I haven't worked it all out yet. But for some time now I have been having your movements watched carefully."

"Why me?"

"Because I care for you and do not wish to see you taken and hung!"

Hanna gasped.

"You are frightening my child," Dora said in a low voice.

"Good. Then perhaps it will bring you to your senses."

"These charges are insane."

"Are they?"

"If you had any proof you'd have me arrested."

"If I saw something going on before my own eyes, Dora, I would be forced to act. Please do not put me in that position. After the wedding, I'll see to it that you get safely home. But I want your sacred promise never to return."

"I'll think about it. Meanwhile, if you don't mind, I'd like to be left alone with my daughter."

"I'd appreciate your answer in the next hour or so," he said. At a snap of his fingers a nearby slave rushed up to take his horse. Then Austin strode off to the house.

Mama knelt beside Hanna. "Darling, there's very little time. Don't cry. Don't speak loudly. We can't know for sure if Rosalie's been captured. Anything could have happened. I have to go right away and look for her. She could be hiding somewhere. Now I musn't take you with me. You understand that, don't you?"

"No, Mama," Hanna sobbed. "I *have* to be with you. My dream meant I've got to be with you!"

"Your dream?"

"I have to save Li'l Rafe!"

"Darling, I doubt if there's any way to help Rosalie's little boy. God alone knows if there's any chance for Rosalie. But I *must* try. I want you to go back to Aunt Ida. Tell her I love her very much. Tell her that if anything goes wrong, she should take you back to Indiana herself. Ask her to keep Austin busy with the wedding preparations so that he doesn't notice I'm gone for as long as possible. Kiss me, my dearest one. That's it. Now off you go."

"Mama, don't leave me!"

"Go now."

As Hanna went back through the pasture gate, she turned to look back at her mother. But Mama was already rushing to the buggy.

A terrible fear struck Hanna's heart that she would never see her mother again. Looking over toward the house, Hanna saw Aunt Ida on the top step. The old lady was staring this way as if wondering what in the world was going on. Hanna lifted her arm. She saw her great-aunt take off her spectacles to see better. Hanna waved good-bye to her, and threw her a kiss with both hands. Then she ran like blazes after Mama.

She saw her mother leading Johnny Appleseed out of his stall to the buggy. How was she going to do this without Mama knowing? The hiding place under the seat! If she could only get past her mother without being seen . . .

A man rushed up to help Dora put the horse in

harness. He was the slave who had taken the other man's horse. Crouching low, Hanna slipped close to them.

"That man don't know we got eyes and ears," he said to Mama as they worked quickly. "Or else he just don't see us till he want us. But God be with you, we suspicioned all along that you was part of the Freedom Train. Your aunt, she be better'n most. But it ain't her go out in the fields with us. The overseer, he tells us what to do. Does anything he wants with anybody. Can you get me away from here? There's others, too. Women folk."

When Mama turned to gently put her hand on his arm, Hanna slipped under the seat.

"But if you heard that my aunt is going to . . . "

"I don't have no faith in what's gonna happen *sometime*. Don't know if I kin wait for that. They's people down here fixin' to find ways to stop everythin'."

"I'll do what I can," Mama said, "but I can't take anybody now. I must go."

Johnny Appleseed wasn't very young and he was never a fast horse, but Mama had never been in such a hurry before. He knew her moods and he knew better than to dawdle. Soon his hooves were flying like a young horse's. And only when it was too late for Mama to turn back did Hanna crawl out and put her arms around her mother's neck.

"I might have known," was all Mama said.

But Hanna knew that she was thinking: Please God you won't have to see your mother die.

TEN

Mama would not let up on Johnny Appleseed. The old horse plunged ahead to the crossroad ten miles farther on, and then made the same turn Rosalie would have made the night before. The new road was little more than a narrow horse path that cut through a dense forest. There were no farms here, and very few shacks.

But farther on there would be a town and the lawyer's office. If Rosalie had managed to escape the trap, she would be somewhere between there and here.

Hanna and Dora looked in all directions for some sign of Rosalie, but nothing moved in the woods. Nor was it possible to see very far ahead on the road. It curved around rocky places and densely grown thickets. That was why they heard the pounding hoofbeats before they saw the runaway horse with the buckboard bouncing wildly behind it. It was coming straight at them, heading for a crash. But before Johnny Appleseed could rear, Mama jerked him quickly to the side. The buggy rolled off the road just in time.

Now came other hoofbeats. Several horses came around the same turn, carrying men with rifles. Mama called out to them and one of them pulled up as the others rode on.

"Anything broke, ma'am? Anyone hurt?"

"No, but I thank you kindly for stopping," Mama said, and gave him a charming smile. "It was so frightening having that riderless wagon come flying at us. Can you tell me, please, what in the world is going on?"

The man touched the tip of his cap politely. "Yes, ma'am. We're after a woman who stole a slave boy last night. We lost her back there somewhere and split up into two parties. If they can't catch her in the woods, we'll find her this way. Leastways we'll find who she's been workin' with. Yonder horse is gonna lead us right to the stable where it was taken from. If I were you, I'd be careful goin' that way. She could be dangerous."

"I thank you again," Mama said, "but I am armed and a very good shot."

He touched his cap a second time, saying "Good day, ma'am," and rode off after the others.

"How am I going to find her if they're patrolling the road?" Mama murmured to herself. "She has to be in hiding now."

"Mama?" Hanna was tugging at her sleeve.

"What?"

"I remember this happening before. The horse and wagon coming. Then the men."

"For heaven's sake, child, are you going to talk to me about that dream *now?*"

"No, Mama. It's not a dream. It's like a . . . a memory."

"Please don't do this when I have to keep my wits about me!" Dora shook the reins and they started off.

"There's gonna be a big flat rock, Mama. With littler rocks spread out on it to look like—"

"I don't know what you're talking about," Mama snapped. "And I don't want you saying anything, you hear? I need to think."

They rode on in silence for a long while, each of them studying the woods. Suddenly, Hanna jumped up in her seat and pointed. "There!"

"I asked you not to—"

"But that's it! The Drinking Gourd!"

"Drinking Gourd?"

"Yes, Mama, don't you remember? That's what you and Rosalie told me runaways follow at night to get north."

"You mean the Big Dipper in the sky? Child, those are just some rocks!"

"No, they aren't just some rocks. Rosalie set them out there like that. Look, that's the handle. And that's the gourd. And . . . Mama, please slow us down. . . ."

Hanna's gaze traveled to the right. Suddenly, she swung her arm over. "There! That rock all the way over there. That's where the North Star's supposed to be. Only this one is a-pointin' at those big boulders back in there. That's where she is with Li'l Rafe! Mama, it's a sign!"

"You could be right," her mother said, staring hard at the rocks. She slowed the buggy. "Now, Hanna, we have to act quickly. I want you to hop off while I go on. The other men may come by and I can't stop here. That could make them take a closer look around. I will go on very slowly till I find a spot where I can let the horse stop for water. Then I'll turn back as if I've been thinking it over and I decided it was too dangerous to go that way with fugitives on the loose. First thing you do is go up to those little rocks and scatter them, in case it gives anybody else ideas. Then get out of sight yourself if you can while you look for them. I don't see how I can possibly fit both Rosalie and her son under the seat. But we'll have to do something. Now scoot."

Hanna ran uphill to the boulder. Her little bridesmaid's dress ripped loudly as she climbed it. She looked back to see Johnny Appleseed pull a mouthful of grass from the roadside before moving on.

Now there were other rocks to climb. Higher and higher she went, skinning her knees. "Rosalie," she called.

But there was no answer—nothing but the squawk of a blue jay.

She called again.

This time it was only a woodpecker's clacking that came back to her.

It was a steeper climb now. She scraped her leg. She was bleeding. That wouldn't have happened if she'd been wearing boy's pantaloons.

Hanna was just about to cry out for Rosalie again when she felt a little breath of air touch the back of her neck. "Girl," whispered a voice in her ear, "don't you know nothin' 'bout Indian calls?"

She whirled around and saw a small black boy of about seven. "Li'l Rafe?"

He grinned at her. "You like how close I kin get without nobody see me?"

"Where's your mama?"

"My mammy's in the cave. She don't want you callin' out like that. Sounds go a long way here."

"Where's the cave?"

"Show you."

He led her behind a boulder, and then around a second one to an opening about the size of a cabin door.

Rosalie sat huddled on the stone floor just inside, a pistol in her lap. She didn't look well. Hanna rushed up to her. "Are you hurt?"

"No, but I had to rest. My heart's been thumpin' and it don't want to slow back down. I'll be fine presently. Where's your mama?"

"She went on a ways but she's comin' back. We'd better go right down."

"Give me just a minute or two more. We've been doin' a lot of runnin'."

"But, Rosalie, why didn't you stay with the horse?"

"That way they'd have caught us for sure. Don't make me talk now."

"Mammy," said Little Rafe. "You ain't gonna die?"

"What? You crazy? After I just found my baby boy? No chance. We gonna to be together forever. Let me be for a minute now."

A low rumbling sound came from the deepness of the tunnel. "What was that?" Hanna asked worriedly. "Is this place gonna fall in?"

Little Rafe only smiled proudly. "No, that's the bear. Big bear live here. But my mammy done chase him to the back part of the cave. He don't like that. He wants us to go. He done roared much louder'n this. But you should hear *my mammy* holler!"

"Really? Or are you making it up?"

"I'm not makin' up nothin'. You ought to see what she done to the master. Fetch him one punch with her fist and he go down. Then my mammy, she tie him up like a hog. Stick an apple in his mouth, too. That was so funny I like to laugh till I died. Then I say, 'You must be Mother Freedom.' And she say, 'Some do call me that. You kin call me your mammy. 'Cause that's who I is.'"

His voice shook. "Couldn't believe that. I done forgot what she look like. Wanted to 'member but I couldn't. Man that bought me, he say my mother was dead! But . . . but she told me close my eyes and listen to her voice. And she 'membered me things I had forgotten."

Little Rafe wiped his eyes with the bottom of his long, hanging shirt. Hanna put a hand on his shoulder. "You didn't know she was comin' for you? They didn't tell you that?"

"They didn't tell me nothin'. 'Cept, 'Boy, you better hurry up some gettin' big and strong. You costin' us money here. By and by we gonna stop feedin' you.'"

Little Rafe brightened. "Mammy say she and me are goin' to school when we get to freedom. She say she been makin' a skinny schoolteacher fat so he teach us, too."

"I'm reading the life of George Washington."

"Is it good?"

"Some of it, I reckon. But I don't believe that he never told a lie. My mama's been tellin' lies all day."

"Slaves has to do it most *all* the time. Else they gets bullwhipped. 'Course they better be good at it. If they gets caught a-lyin', they gets bullwhipped even hard—"

"I'm ready," announced Rosalie, wobbling to her feet.

The buggy was waiting below when they climbed down from the rocks. "Rosalie," said Mama, "you look deathly ill."

"I'm fine," said Rosalie quickly. "Give me room to get in under there."

"There's not enough room—"

"I know that," Rosalie interrupted. "You take Li'l Rafe with you up there. Keep him in the middle. You got your gun? Hold it on him like he's a big, desperate black man. And don't try to get away from them slavers. Turn *to* them. It's the only way to do it, you understand?"

"Of course I understand," Mama scolded. "I had the same idea myself, but you're being so bossy."

"Li'l Rafe? Tell that white woman who the boss is here."

"My mammy!"

"All right, I'm in. This is some fit. I ain't never gonna be able to stand up again. Now this piece of cloth ain't enough, if anybody wants to look close down here. Where's that hay that's suppose to be coverin' the front of me?"

"It's down here at my feet. Hanna was hiding in there and it got scattered when she came—" Mama interrupted herself. "I swear, if I'm not defending myself to Aunt Ida, I'm doing it to you!"

Hanna looked at her mother and realized that this wasn't a quarrel at all. The two women were just trying to keep up their own courage and their children's.

They had not been on the road long when Hanna said, "They're a-comin' now."

Mama lifted her head. "I don't hear anything. Do you?"

"No, but over yonder in the woods, the men are gonna be comin' out from behind that weeping willow."

"Look, you made a very good guess about those rocks. Don't tell me you're still imagining you were here before."

"Mama, I *was* here before." She turned to Little Rafe. "Everythin' went fine, Li'l Rafe."

Rosalie's muffled voice came through the straw. "Rafe! Act scared."

"I *is* scared, Mammy."

"I mean like you're real scared of Hanna's mama."

As Johnny Appleseed pulled the loaded buggy along, a line of men began to appear. They looked mean, probably because they were having so much trouble finding Rosalie. Spreading out along the side of the road, each of them held his horse's reins in one hand. In the other, he held his rifle upright on his knee, fingers already on the trigger.

"This the little boy who you're looking for?" Mama sang out merrily.

"Could be," one of the men said darkly. "What's his name?"

"Not sure if I heard him rightly, he's been trembling so. But I believe he said Little Rafe."

"That's him, all right," said the man. "My

compliments, ma'am. You did a good job. We'll take him now."

"You most certainly will not!" Mama snorted indignantly. "Look at my little girl's dress. That was her going-to-a-wedding dress. You have any idea what it took me to make that? Now I don't have time to make another. I'll have to *buy* one."

"I don't see what that has to do . . . "

"You *don't*? How do you think it got all torn like that? My daughter caught him. Did it all by herself actually. Chased him through the woods like a hound after a hare. She is such a brave girl. Threw him down and caught him. And look what it did to her best dress. Look at her knees, too! Why, they're still bleeding. It's going to cost me for the doctor, too. I am taking him back to his master, and I am going to insist on being paid my expenses for this. You would think the man would take better care to keep his property from getting away from him. I'm almost willing to wager that he doesn't belong to any one of you brave gentlemen."

"No, ma'am. Squire Douglas had a bit of a heart attack after that woman hit him in the chest with a blacksmith's hammer."

"With a hammer! Why, that's terrible. But I'm still going to ask him to pay for my child's dress."

"Where's that woman at, boy?" said the man, cutting the conversation short. Leaning forward in his saddle, he gave Little Rafe a fierce, hate-filled look.

"I . . . I . . ."

"He don't know," Hanna said suddenly. "He fell asleep and woke up, and she was gone."

Mama gave her daughter a quick look. "Yes, indeed, that's right. She abandoned him. Can you picture a woman who *says* she's a mother and does a thing like that? They were hiding in a cave some miles back. You can't miss it. There's a big flat rock on the right, and other rocks going up behind it. Now good day, gentlemen. I wish you all the luck you deserve in catching her."

"Oh, we'll catch her," said the man. "And when we do . . ." Patting a rope that was tied around his saddle horn, he galloped off with the others.

When they were out of sight, Rosalie pushed away some of the straw and took a few big gulps of air. "Li'l Rafe, you all right?"

"Mammy!" he cried. "Are we goin' back to Squire Douglas's farm?"

"'Course not. Dora, there's a deer track a small ways down. Might just be wide enough for the buggy to get through till we hit some other road to take us north. Wagon couldn't make it."

"Why didn't you get rid of the wagon and both ride the horse?"

"First off, I don't know *how* to ride a horse. Also, there was no place to hide the wagon. Soon as they found it, they'd come gallopin' right after us. 'Sides which, I figured you'd come after me."

Mama nodded. "I don't see how we can go back to the ferry. They'll be watching it."

"No, we'd best try the Quakers. Maybe they can figure some way to get us out of Kentucky."

Farther along, they came to the trail—or what was left of it. They turned into the forest, and from there on it was slow going. Even at its best, the path was a narrow squeeze for the buggy. But there were parts of it that were blocked by fallen branches, and other places so overgrown with prickly thornbushes that Johnny Appleseed refused to go ahead until they were cleared away.

No one thought of talking until they had been traveling for a long time. There was still no reason to feel safe. But at last Mama said, "As long as we don't shout, I see no reason why we can't make conversation."

What she and Hanna really wanted to hear, of course, was all about the rescue of Little Rafe.

"It was a good thing I didn't wait for mornin' 'fore leavin' your aunt's place," Rosalie began. "No one was expectin' me to come the night before, or to be ridin' into town on a buckboard haulin' sacks of taters like some slave woman workin' real late to make a delivery for her master. So bold as you please, if I do say so, I come ridin' down the middle of the road till I make out the lawyer's office. I was lucky 'cause he was still there. I go through the door and see him tipped back in his seat, boots up on the desk. He say to me, 'We closed. What you want?'

"I say, 'Beg your pardon, Lawyer Griswold. But my master sent me to make certain sure there ain't gonna be no problem 'bout the money to buy Li'l Rafe. Master wants to know when do he get to keep the money Mr. Terwilliger done sent down for him.'

"Lawyer Griswold looked at me mighty funny then. His little piggy eyes get all scrunched together.

"'See here now!' he say. 'I'm gettin' mighty tired of explainin' the same thing over and over to the squire. Terwilliger mailed the money to me because I drew up the contract for the sale of that slave. The law says I've got to hold onto the money until the property gets turned over to its new buyer. Only in this case there ain't gonna be a sale. All this is just to catch the mother. When she shows up in the mornin', she's gonna be arrested 'fore she steps one foot into this office. We are gonna have sheriff's men hidin' in my closet and up on the roof and in every other place they can think of. Then she's gonna be questioned real careful till she confesses to agitatin', stealin', and smugglin' out other slaves. Now I've explained this to him several times before. But between you and me, your master is too stupid to hold anything in his head for five minutes altogether. Do you think you can drill it back into him?'

"'Shore will try,' I told the lawyer. 'Thank you, suh.' And I headed for the door.

"I get in my buckboard and head out to the place where my boy was. I snuck over to the slave cabins, where I found Li'l Rafe. Knowed him at once. He was sittin' outside on a stump under the moonlight, a-cryin' and a-cryin'. Seems like the master done told him for the first time that his mother wasn't dead. But he'd said that tomorrow, when I come for him, there'd be a lynchin'.

"I didn't get to find out none of that right off, 'cause a dog had set up a-howlin' when I come in. The master come rollin' out of his back door in his sleepin' clothes to yell, 'Hush that racket!' That's when I step up in front of him. Don't know where I got the strength from, 'cause he was big. But all I could think of was how hungry-lookin' my boy was, and I whopped him so hard he fall like a stone. Then I turn to my boy, who I ain't seen in five solid years.

"'Li'l Rafe,' I say to him real low. 'I'm your mammy, come to get you. Can you find me some rope real quick so we can get out of here?' And that was it."

"Were you crying, too?" Mama asked softly.

"Surely would have been nice. But I didn't have no time for it. Not till we got to the cave, and by then I was tuckered out." Little Rafe was sitting beside her and she turned his face toward hers. "But now I got the time." Her voice broke. "All the time there is."

Hanna watched their arms go around each other until Dora took her daughter's hand and squeezed it. It was a moment or so before she understood. Then she looked away to let Rosalie and Little Rafe be alone together.

Some time later, Hanna piped up. "Rosalie, what was it you hit that man with?"

"It were her *fist*!" Little Rafe insisted. "And it were in the *face*! What else was the squire gonna tell them men? He wasn't gonna say, 'It was a woman done it to me with her one hand.'"

Mama laughed. "Rosalie, your son takes to freedom pretty quick."

"Why not?" came the answer. "He sure been needin' it long enough."

ELEVEN

The trail came to an end near the bottom of a hill. Everybody saw at once that there was no way to continue with the buggy.

Mama heaved a sigh. But it was she who got off first and unhitched Johnny Appleseed. Had he been a mule instead of a horse, it would have been easier for him to make the climb. They had to go sideways up the slope—all four of them tugging him along—until he made it to the top.

Near the top they came to a flatter, grassy place. The grown-ups were out of breath. Rosalie sank against a tree, sweating heavily. It was hard for her to pay attention to the important question that her son suddenly raised.

"Mammy, I ain't so little. Why everyone call me *Li'l* Rafe?"

"'Cause your pappy," Rosalie panted, "he was *Big* Rafe."

"Where is my pappy now?"

"He got sold off 'fore you, son. I tracked him down into Mississippi 'bout a year ago. But he died. I'm sorry."

The boy hung his head for a moment. Then he said, "Then I'm Big Rafe now. Can you call me that?"

"Why don't I just call you—"

Hanna interrupted them. She had gone ahead a few dozen yards to the top. Now she hurried halfway back with the news. "I just saw the river!"

Following her, they all peered down through the trees. The two women looked at each other and frowned.

"Do you know this part of the country, Dora?"

"Yes. Well, more or less I do," said Mama, "from passing by on the steamboat. But I'm afraid we've come out much too far west to ever make it safely to the Quakers."

"That's all right," bragged Rafe. "My mammy gonna get us across."

"Listen to that boy. He thinks if I flapped my arms, I'd fly like an eagle."

"No, mammy, look!" Rafe pointed to a small raft in the distance that was being brought to shore.

Rosalie squinted. "Never could see good that far. How many men on it?"

"I'm so nearsighted myself, I can't see a thing," said Mama. "Left my specs at Aunt Ida's."

"Two men!" cried Rafe. "They tyin' it up. Now they goin' into that shed."

Hanna had half seen, half heard. But something in her had drifted off. She was becoming lost in memories—or dreams. It was almost as if she was running away from being right there, right then.

There was something about Little Rafe—about *Rafe*, she had to call him now—that made her want to cry, or run away from him. She was starting to like him.

Mama, meanwhile, was very worried. "We could run into another one of those longboats," she said. "They'd surely be looking for us this time." She glanced up at the sky. "Well, it's cloudy, at least, and that's a blessing. I forget whether there's going to be a moon tonight."

"No moon," said Rosalie. "But I don't see how we can just stay here a-waitin' for the sun to go down. If you ask me, those slavers that are after us must have put it all together long ago. And if they found the wagon tracks on the trail, they be a-headin' this way for sure."

Mama nodded. "Neither of us see any perfect answer. So why don't we do the best we can? We'll go as far as we can and still be able to find some place to hide until it gets real dark."

Down the slope they all went, until Rafe said he smelled smoke. It was a few minutes more before they saw the top of the small chimney from where it came. Moving more carefully now, they came to the edge of a small farm.

Now it was Johnny Appleseed's turn to sniff the air. But it wasn't the scent of fire that interested him. Lifting his head, he gave a loud whinny. Another whinny answered him, and a big spotted mare came storming out of her stall. Hanna tried to tighten her grip on the bridle. But it was too much for a ninety-pound girl to control a one-thousand-pound, just-fallen-in-love horse. Johnny Appleseed pulled away from her like an unleashed lightning bolt.

A woman came racing from the barn with a pitchfork. What she meant to do with it, no one could be sure. When she saw the fallen Hanna, and the others at the edge of the woods, she stood there in wonderment.

Rosalie stepped into the field with her pistol drawn. "Put that down and don't move," she ordered.

The pitchfork stayed where it was. And the woman looked at her without fear. "If you're a-fixin' to shoot me, go ahead," she said. "But this is *my* land. And it's gonna be on your immortal soul that you done left three children motherless."

"Believe me, we're not looking to harm anybody," said Mama, putting a hand on Rosalie's arm.

But Rosalie was looking mean. Hanna had never seen her look that way. Was it because Rosalie was feeling so sick? "Where's your husband?" Rosalie asked.

"Come down with the fever and died last year. You're a-standin' where he's buried. Watch out for that cross now. You knock it over and that gun ain't a-gonna stop me."

Rosalie stepped around the two nailed-together logs. "So you ain't just the farmer's wife," she said, wiping her face and breathing hard. "You the farmer."

"That's right. Got somethin' against that?"

"No, I don't." Rosalie squinted hard at her. "I suppose you *think* you know who we is?"

"Don't know. Don't care to know. I keep to my farm. And I mind my business."

"This here is my son," said Rosalie, softening. "He was a slave. They was a-starvin' him. I tried to buy him free, but they was gonna trick me. So I took him."

The farmer nodded. "I kin understand that. Do the same myself."

"So you don't hold with slavery then?" Mama asked hopefully.

There was a long silence. "No, I never liked it," the farmer said at last. "They try to say that slavery's in the Bible. But in the Bible the children of Israel got themselves away from it, though it took them forty years. So I don't see how the Lord kin favor it."

"Amen," said Rosalie, putting aside her gun.

"Amen," said the farmer, studying her closely. "You look poorly."

"I'm fine."

"Well, if you say so." She turned to the others. "Y'all hungry? Don't have much to give you. Some ham and hominy. But you're all a-welcome."

Hanna's stomach had long been growling. She was all set to run to the cabin, but her mother gave her a look. "We surely appreciate that," she said. "But if you have children in there, it might not be wise. They might be questioned later. I think it would be better for you if they didn't know you were kind to us."

"But if we hold a gun on you," Rosalie suggested in a tired voice, "it might scare your young'uns."

"Tain't nothin' kin scare them 'cept me," said the farmer. " 'Sides, they're over to a barn raisin', and they gonna stay the night. Now if you got no more excuses, come on inside."

After everyone had eaten, Rosalie asked if she could lie down for a bit. The woman let her climb up into a crawl space where the children slept. Rosalie barely set her head down before she fell asleep. Rafe wanted to lie beside her, but Hanna impatiently snatched his hand away from the ladder.

"Will you give her a chance, Kevin, and just let her rest?"

"*Kevin?*" he snorted. "Girl, who's that? My name is *Rafe*."

"I . . . well, that's what I meant. Look, you leave me alone."

"Fine and dandy. When did I bother you in the first place? Answer me that, Miss High and Mighty!"

Mama threw a scolding look across the small floor. She caught Hanna's eyes and shook her head slowly. Hanna barely managed to cover her face before she burst into tears.

In another moment, Hanna had her arms tightly

around her mother. The farmer made a motion toward the boy.

Shyly, Rafe got up from his chair and walked slowly over to her. She put a hand on his hair, let it slide down to the back of his head, and drew him to her. "Your mammy's gonna be all right," she said, rocking him gently. "Jesus loves a woman that fights for her son. Everything's a-gonna be just fine. You want to come up and sit on my lap now?"

And Rafe, with his eyes glistening and his face buried in the woman's neck, gulped down his sobs and nodded.

Time passed. The flame in the oil lamp had long ago been blown out. Hanna, sitting in a chair by herself, awakened with a start from another of her troubling dreams. Her mother was awake, too, keeping watch through a crack in the door. Rafe had been sleeping in the farmer's arms, but now the woman woke him gently and told him to go fetch his mammy.

"They all be a-sleepin' like the dead down by the river now," she explained to Hanna's mother.

Mrs. Terwilliger nodded and thanked her with a little embrace. "If there's anything I can ever do for you . . . " she said.

"Well, I was a-thinkin'," began the farmer slowly.

"Yes?"

"Ain't likely that your horse is 'bout to leave my mare without a lot of fussin' and her a-callin' after him when he goes. All that whinnyin' back and forth's a-gonna be noticed by somebody, even in the dark."

Hanna's mother was silent for a moment. "You're right of course. Besides, we owe you so much . . . "

What? thought Hanna. Give away Johnny Appleseed? She sprung to her feet, but her mother gave her another one of her warning looks.

"Pshaw! You don't owe me nothin'. But come plantin' time, if I got me two horses, 'stead of one a-pullin' the plow . . . "

"We want you to have him," Mama said.

"You're sure now?"

Mama clasped the farmer's hands in hers. "Won't take no for an answer."

"Well, then. That's done!" said the woman with relief.

But Hanna wasn't done. "How are you gonna explain if someone asks how you got him?" she snapped.

"That's not a problem," her mother put in sternly. "All anybody will think is that we set the horse free because we couldn't take him with us. Which is *true*, Hanna. After that, Johnny Appleseed could have wandered here. It's easy to understand why. He's going to be very happy here."

Now the two women were grinning at each other.

It was a secret sort of grin. "He's found a horse he wants to marry."

They had been offered a lantern but didn't take it. They were glad for the blackness of the night. But the winding path that led away from the farm was full of ruts and holes, and it was hard not to stumble and fall. To keep from losing one another, they held hands. And it was Rafe, with his wonderful eyesight, who led the way.

They knew they were getting closer to the river when a strong breeze whipped through the trees to strike their faces. But they got no glimpse of it even when the rugged and twisting path came to an end in a smoother road of packed-down dirt. Dark and silent houses began to appear on both sides of them. They were coming into a sleeping town, and their greatest fear now was of barking dogs. But it was cats that watched them with glowing eyes, cats as silent as the front yard fences they perched on .

It was beginning to thunder now. Suddenly, a candle flared in an upstairs room. A man with a nightcap on his head came to the open window and looked their way. They all stopped at once. Did he see them? Should they run? Tilting his head, the man stared up at the sky. Then he blew out his candle and closed the window.

They moved on. The road began to slope toward the

riverbank. They were going past what might have been a general store. Then came a big warehouse. They heard the bumping sounds of little boats driftting against the dock to which they were tied. Their feet left the dirt street to step on creaking wooden boards. They could hear the water lapping as they carefully felt their way along, one small step at a time.

One of the boats still had oars in it. Rosalie stepped down first and went to the back. Then the children came down to her. Mama was last. She untied the rope and pushed at the dock. The boat floated away.

Rosalie began to pull at the oars, but Mama went over and took them from her, whispering, "You're still not well. I want you to rest."

Crouching in the front with Rafe, Hanna listened to the thunder and watched her mother strain at the oars. After a while Hanna got up and went over to her. "Let me help you row, Mama."

"No," Mama said in a voice that was firm and weary at the same time. "And don't stand up in a boat."

Hanna started to go back. Then she turned around, ducked under her mother's arms, and dropped onto the slat beside her. "I am gonna help you and that is that." She grabbed hold of one of the oars.

For a moment she thought Mama would scold her. Instead she felt a pair of lips on her cheek. "I declare, child, you're beginning to sound just like Aunt Ida."

Hanna was pleased. But she soon had trouble

matching Mama's strength with her own. The boat kept turning in her direction.

"Girl, you a mess. Move over," said Rafe, coming over to cram in beside her.

"Wish I knew who you remind me of," Hanna muttered with annoyance.

All of a sudden the sky lit up. A great zigzag of lightning flashed across the sky.

And there was a longboat, coming straight at them!

"Halt!" someone shouted. "Y'all stay right there! Or we'll fire!"

Rosalie sat up, her face covered with sweat. "Oh, Lord, not *here*. Not now, when we so close!"

"Ship them oars!" boomed the voice. "Take them out of the water. Do like I say, right now!"

It came too quickly for anyone to realize what was happening, but they all saw it. Another white flash—this one shooting over their heads—and a great sizzle of blue flame in the longboat. The men had drawn the lightning with their rifles. A sharp burning smell mixed with the screams of terrified men, and the broken boat overturned.

Then there was darkness again. Men called to one another as they swam. Others clung to floating bits of wreckage.

"Don't stop for nobody," Rosalie warned. "You knows what will happen if any of them get into this boat!"

Mama and the children rowed away quickly. Soon heavy rain began to fall, splashing the river and soaking them. But at long last there was the sliding sound of wood touching mud and rock. Together they all beached the boat, and then closed around one another in a giant hug. Rosalie sent up a whoop of joy. And Mama's good spirits burst out all over her face.

"Take hands," she said, opening out the circle. And—soaked from head to foot in the pouring rain—they did a little dance on freedom's shore.

TWELVE

They had landed just before dawn, but when the sun rose, it was hidden behind the dark rain clouds. As they trudged along, Rosalie said she was glad it was still storming. "This way won't be so many on the road."

They were many miles from home, yet Rosalie knew the town they were approaching. She said it was a dangerous place, not only for runaways but for freed blacks, as well. There had been many stories of others coming across the river at night. Only these were slave catchers. They would break into homes of sleeping black folks and kidnap them at gunpoint.

"Don't matter if you got papers to show you free," she explained in a low voice, as they hurried along the back streets. "They puts a gag in your mouth and chains on your arms and legs, and they takes you back over. You never be seen again."

She led them to a two-room cabin that had been turned into a church. The door was closed and no one answered her knock. Finally, she put her mouth to a crack in the door, saying, "Pastor, this is a voice I thinks you know."

They heard a bolt being pulled and saw a small,

bearded black man. Gazing at Rosalie, he broke into a smile.

"Welcome, Mother Freedom! Do come in. It's a sad day when a house of worship has to be locked up tight, but things have gotten much worse here since I saw you last."

He paused to look at the others, but said nothing. "Forgive me I don't introduce them, Pastor," said Rosalie. "But as usual, the less you know the better."

He held up a hand. "You don't have to explain. I understand. My, my, but you all look half drowned. While I put on some tea, why don't you all take a place by the fire?"

"Thank you, Pastor," said Mama, as they followed him through the church into a small back room. "You say it's gotten worse here lately. How is that?"

He looked at Dora again.

"She work with me sometime," Rosalie explained.

"Indeed?" he said, smiling at Mama now. "Yet you sound as if you come from the Southland yourself. A very soft and sweet Virginia accent, if I'm not mistaken."

"Well, that's my aunt's doing. She drilled it into me. Actually, I was raised in Kentucky."

He nodded. "Well, there are many people who don't hold with slavery in Kentucky. I have hopes for that state. Were you raised among slaves?"

"Yes, I was."

"You've seen the lash being used?"

"Not on my father's land. But, of course, I knew of it."

The pastor sighed. "No white person from a slave-owning family ever seems to remember the lash being used on his or her own property."

Hanna saw her mother's cheeks grow red. "My aunt has the farm now," she said. "I truly doubt if she's ever seen it used." Then her voice dropped. "But I also agree that it probably has been there. I hope to do something about that soon."

"It pleases me to hear you say so," said the pastor. "Ah, here's your tea. Forgive me if I have no saucers for your cups, or if you see a crack or two along the rim. My flock cannot afford to pay me very well. And now there are so many less of them."

"Black folks here'bouts are finally leavin'?" asked Rosalie.

"Oh yes. They tried to hold out. But now they're taking whatever they can carry and running for their lives. Trying to get to Canada. They don't think our people will be safe anywhere in America now. Not with this new fugitive law coming in. A black person won't even be able to go to court to prove that he or she is a free person. Two white people just have to swear to a lie that a black person is a runaway, and the black person will be arrested. He'll be taken in front of a special judge. He can't ask this judge to have a jury try his case. Why, he won't even be allowed to tell his own story on the witness stand, or prove that he was a free man all along. And even if some white person wants to testify for him, the judge has a very good reason not to believe the truth anyway. He gets paid for each person he delivers into slavery. Wait, here is what Frederick Douglass, our dear brother in the struggle, has written about this law in his newspaper." Taking a copy of the *North Star* from a table, he read: "'On the oath of any two villains a free man can be made a slave for life!'"

Rafe's eyes had been widening as he listened to the pastor. He turned to his mother. "I thought I was free!"

"Nobody is free till we all free," Rosalie replied. "But I ain't gonna let anyone get you. Never again, my honey. I promise you that. Anyone who tries it, I kills him first." She turned to the pastor. "You'd best keep a shotgun here yourself, case they come for you. But look here. We need to get on our way without bein' seen. Kin you help us?"

"I'll see what I can do while you're drying out." Taking a wide-brimmed hat and an old coat from a hook, the pastor went to the door. He stopped to look back at Rosalie.

"I'll tell you what saves me from the kidnappers. It's the fact that I can read and write. The last black person any owner wants to buy is one who can educate his other slaves."

"Maybe so," said Rosalie. "But killin' you is somethin' else!"

The pastor shrugged as he opened the door. "The Lord will decide what happens."

"No, Reverend. It ain't always the Lord what decides who is to be hung from a tree."

He sighed before he left. "I do believe you put me in mind of Sojourner Truth, our beloved sister from New York. May she continue to be a voice for us all wherever we are. And you the spark of justice. Amen."

"Amen," said Mama fervently, and smiled with love at Rosalie.

Rafe tugged at his mother's skirt. "Mammy, what is a 'spark of justice'?"

"Hush now," she answered softly. "Dry yourself and rest. You gonna be a spark yourself soon enough."

While they were waiting, Hanna grew curious about the newspaper. Picking it up, she noticed that it was published in someplace called Rochester, New York.

There was something about that name, as if she'd heard it before. *Rochester?* It must have been a city. Yet why did it make her think of a little field, a field covered with blue cornflowers?

Hanna really didn't feel much like reading, but she took the paper with her to the edge of the parson's bed and sat. Her eyes skimmed down the front page.

In one place the names of people at a meeting were mentioned. One of the names gave her another strange feeling. *Post.* It seemed to her as if she both knew and didn't know the name of Isaac Post.

And look, down here the article mentioned Amos Terwilliger . . . *Papa?* It said he'd written a letter because he couldn't be there, and the letter was read out loud to everybody. Papa's letter, think of that! He'd had some things to say about the Fugitive Slave Act, too. But Hanna's lids had grown heavy by then. She let the paper drift to her lap and fell asleep.

When she awakened, it was time to go. A horse and covered wagon were waiting outside the door. The cloth on the back of the wagon was rolled up, and the wagon seemed to be filled with great chunks of ice.

"I'm afraid you're not going to be very warm in there," the pastor said as they climbed in over the ice and ducked out of sight under some rags. "My flock can't afford to pay me much for being their pastor," he explained as he climbed into the driver's seat. "So I have to earn my living doing other things, as well. One of them is making deliveries for a white man who produces ice in a cave. This is going to be a delivery I shall treasure all my life."

Even with such a trusted friend as the pastor, Mother Freedom had to be careful. She knew that no one could torture her into revealing secrets. But it was better not to expect that of anyone else. She had never told the pastor about the hotel, and now she had him drop them off about ten miles from it.

A whole day had passed since they'd started out, and it was dark as they walked along the side of the road. Even when the hotel was in sight, they waited until all the lights had gone out. Then Mama slipped inside to see if all was well. After a few minutes, she waved to the others, who were crouched among the trees. Hanna, with her torn clothing, came next, still clutching the newspaper. The pastor had let her take it to show Papa. Then came Rosalie, walking slowly.

Hanna looked outside and couldn't see Rafe. Had Rosalie hidden him? And as soon as Rosalie came through the doorway, Hanna whispered, "Why did you leave Rafe behind?"

"Use your head, child," said Mama. "Some guest could be looking out of a window."

"And who say I left him behind?" muttered Rosalie, lifting her wide skirts. "Take another look."

THIRTEEN

It was three days now since twelve-year-old Anna Post had disappeared. Her parents were frantic with fear and worry. The police told them that they could not stay at the closed hotel, so they took a room in town. But Allan insisted on returning to the hotel every day.

"I can't explain why I have to go back there," he'd told Barbara. "But the clues are in that place. I know it. I just feel it! And it has something to do with the past."

Barbara couldn't stand to be there herself, not after what had happened. Instead she took little Kevin to the town library. She pulled down from the shelves any books about the past that seemed as if they might mention the Terwilligers. She found several mentions of Dora and Amos Terwilliger being abolitionists in the days before the Civil War. There was even a drawing of the hotel in one of the books. It was believed, the author had written, that runaway slaves had sometimes been hidden there. But no one had ever been able to prove it.

The Terwilligers would never talk about it, not even years later after President Lincoln had freed the slaves in the rebellious states. They had lost their daughter during the early days of the Underground Railroad, and they did not wish to dwell on painful memories.

Barbara looked carefully for any mention of a secret tunnel, but she could not find it anywhere.

When she showed the book to Allan, he phoned the chief of police. "I've been thinking about the tunnel coming out by the gravestone," he said. "I couldn't get all the way through because it was caved in, but it's got to lead to a secret room. I've been all over that hotel and couldn't find it. But if we dig out the rest of the tunnel . . . "

"Forget it," said the chief. "It was enough that we opened the grave. And I wouldn't advise you to do it on your own."

But that was exactly what Allan Post did. He returned with a small shovel and flashlight and crawled back into the pit.

It was almost impossible to work in that narrow space. And where was he going to put the dirt? He had to pass it beneath his body and pile it up behind him.

But there was great danger in that. The more earth he dug out in front of him, the more he closed off the tunnel in back of him. If he didn't leave *some* space there, he could cut off his air supply. And what if he came to a dead end? Would he have enough strength to turn around and dig himself out again?

On he went anyway. He had to find Anna!

At last he came to the little opening at the end of the tunnel. Pushing away more dirt, he slithered through it like a snake and landed on a cold stone floor.

The air was dank and musty, and there was deep blackness all around him. Getting to his feet, he pressed the button on his flashlight, but the battery was almost dead. He glanced around the room and saw a lantern on a table. Would it light?

He flicked on his cigarette lighter and noticed that the flame seemed to be touched by a little breeze. Looking up, he saw a small pipe leading from the ceiling. Allan lit the lantern and looked around.

He saw a sleeping mat on the floor and a book on the table next to the place where the lantern had been. He looked at the cover. It was a book about the life of George Washington, by a parson named Weems.

A quill pen lay beside the book. Allan opened the book and saw that someone had written on the first page.

> This here be my gift to Rafe
> But he better learn it
> And keep it safe

It was signed *Hanna Terwilliger*.

The more Allan stared at the writing, the more he felt the flesh on his back begin to prickle and rise.

"It's as if my Anna wrote this," he whispered to himself in astonishment. "This is *her* handwriting!"

Allan climbed the rickety ladder to the trapdoor in the ceiling and tried to open it, but it wouldn't budge.

Again and again he pressed against it, using all his strength. Still no good!

Maybe he could break it open. Going down the ladder, he returned with the shovel. The blade broke when he struck it against the wood. Now he had no way of digging back out through the tunnel. He tried banging with the handle. The handle broke, too.

But then the door above began to move. It opened, and Allan saw Barbara standing above him with the chief of police.

They pulled him up into a narrow hallway. "Am I under arrest?" Allan asked the chief.

"No, but your wife got worried and I drove her out. First we went down to the cemetery, and then we came here. We heard you banging, and moved this rug. I guess someone put a dressing table over it long ago."

"Wait a minute," said Allan. Going back down into the hidden room, he returned with the book. "Barbara, look in here. Is this Anna's handwriting or not?"

"Well, I suppose it looks like it," she said.

"Looks like it? Only *looks*?"

"Well, it's very much like the way she wrote when she was younger."

"But, Barbara, that little girl was missing when she was nine years old!"

"Allan, I think this is a bit crazy."

"Daddy," said Kevin, who had come along, too. "Did you have somebody in your family named Isaac?"

"My grandfather. Why?"

"And was his wife named Amy?"

"No."

"Oh," said the little boy, disappointed.

"Why do you ask?"

Kevin showed him the book he'd taken from the children's section of the library. It was about a woman whose name was Sojourner Truth. She had been born into slavery. Later she traveled from place to place to convince white people to put an end to its horrors. And she had become very friendly with a white woman named Amy Post. The book said that Amy and Isaac Post used to smuggle slaves to Canada from their home in Rochester, New York.

Allan looked for a chair on which to sit down. He found one in the Terwilligers' bedroom. "I suppose my grandfather could have been named Isaac after his own dad or granddad," he said. "I never learned much about the people in my family. I was very small when my parents died. Later, I looked up a few things, but . . . "

He had stopped talking because of a newspaper on a wall. It was in a glass frame. The newspaper was called the *North Star*, and it was published in Rochester. There was an article in it. It talked about a big meeting against the Fugitive Slave Act. Among the famous speakers was one who was not so well-known. His name was Isaac Post. Near the bottom, there was mention of a letter of support written by an Amos Terwilliger.

"Post and Terwilliger," Allan exclaimed. "They knew each other. At least they knew of each other!"

"Allan, get hold of yourself!" Barbara demanded. "What is the matter with you?"

"The matter is that if Anna went back to the past—"

"She didn't go back."

"Listen. We don't know where she came from. Look how hard we tried to find out without getting any answer."

"Allan, these things just don't happen."

"How do we know they don't? And how can we be sure she didn't return to the time she came from? Didn't she tell me that she thought she knew this place? What scares me is this: If Anna went back to the past, then she'll *die* in the past. Maybe she escaped her fate then, but something must be drawing her to it. Everything we've read shows that after she was taken by slave hunters, the girl's family never found their Hanna alive again. The past can't be altered. Barbara, she'll be murdered!"

Little Kevin covered his ears. In spite of how jealous of his sister he often was, he was terribly afraid for her. "No!" he screamed, running from the room. "No, no, no!"

"Now look what you've done!" stormed Barbara, racing out after their little boy.

Allan Post stood there, feeling as if his whole family was coming apart.

FOURTEEN

No sooner was Rafe smuggled safely down into the hidden room than Rosalie began to sweat again. She just barely made it back up the ladder when her hand went to her chest. "Just need a lie down," she mumbled, staggering to her bed in the room next to Hanna's.

Papa wasted no time riding off to fetch a doctor he trusted.

After examining Rosalie, the doctor said that her heartbeat was irregular. He ordered her to stay in bed for the next couple of weeks. When she scowled, he pointed a finger at Mama, saying, "Don't even let her think of doing anything exciting."

After he left, Rosalie said that the doctor meant well but didn't know his business. He was used to giving his advice to white folks who maybe had the money or the time to take it. But back home there were special teas the slaves would make out of roots—a different root for whatever different thing ailed you. They used boneset tea for colds, red oak bark with alum for sore throats, and scurvy grass for stomach troubles.

On the far end of the next town there lived a hundred-year-old black lady who knew all about herbs and teas. She'd been brought over from Africa on a slave ship. Some said the ship's captain freed her after she cured him of something. Others said it was because he was afraid of her "powers." They called her the Conjure Woman, and Rosalie asked Mama to buy from her what was needed.

Mama had her doubts, but Rosalie said that these remedies worked. They had to, because no slave driver would let any sick slave lie around very long, waiting to get well. "You didn't come out of that cabin bright and early to go to work, he come in after you with that bullwhip and make you wish you died."

When they were alone, Mama told Hanna that she thought it was only Rosalie's "wishful thinking." But the next morning they hitched Papa's riding horse to a buckboard and drove off to find the Conjure Woman.

She lived in a little shanty, and she was so bent over that she was smaller than Hanna. "It's arthritis did that," Mama whispered irritably. "She certainly didn't cure *herself*."

"But she's over a hundred years old!"

"And who knows if *that's* the truth?"

There was no arguing with Mama at a time like this. But Hanna wanted to believe what Rosalie believed. Maybe that's what made the old woman catch her eye. Her look gave Hanna the shivers. Not that it was a frightening stare. It was just . . . quiet.

The way a person might look at the page of a book she was reading.

Hanna felt as if this toothless old woman was *reading* her. She felt she had to stand still, and she did.

Mama was upset about not getting the old woman's attention. She'd tried to tell her about Rosalie's symptoms, but it was as if she was talking to herself. She said something impatiently, but the Conjure Woman kept reading Hanna.

Her toothless mouth opened at last. "You done been here 'fore, child. I 'members you."

"Whatever are you talking about?" Mama demanded.

But the old woman seemed only to notice Hanna. "This happen 'fore. Same. Just the same. Does you know this ain't the first time? Does you know you come back?"

Hanna felt her skin tingling. "I . . . I . . . "

"You knows it. Yes, you does. Not all the way. But—"

"Hanna, I've had enough. We're going." Mama snatched her daughter's hand.

"Wait. I gives you the med'cine for Mother Freedom."

Mama looked at her sharply. "Why do you call Mrs. Sims that?"

"Been through this 'fore," said the Conjure Woman, going into her shanty. "So has you." Moments later she returned with the tea in a little muslin sack.

Mama shakily opened her little money purse. "How much do I owe you?"

"Not now," said the old woman. "The time is almost up. Hold tight to your precious one now. And when you needs me . . . "

Mama yanked Hanna's hand and hurried her to the buckboard. "Crazy woman," she mumbled to herself. "*Crazy* woman!"

But Mama's face had gone pale. She shook the reins too hard. And when Hanna asked what was wrong, all her mother did was cry.

Halfway home, Mama wiped her eyes. By the time they drove up to the hotel, she was saying, "I don't know what's got into me. I truly don't." She gave a nervous little laugh. "It was all so silly. But when that woman said those things, I thought I was going to lose you. That's the sort of thing these tricksters do—white or black—who try to sell you on foolishness. It's just so you'll come back to them and keep giving them money."

"But she didn't take any money from you."

"That," huffed Mama, "is just the way they rope you in! But no more talk of it. The whole thing is forgotten. Completely forgotten, right?"

Hanna was silent.

"Right, Hanna? We don't want to upset your father with this nonsense."

"Yes, Mama."

* * *

An hour after taking the tea, Rosalie announced that she was cured. Then she started to get up—and fell right back down on the bed.

Hanna noticed that Mama looked almost glad. Not that her mother didn't want Rosalie to get better—of course, she wanted that with all her heart and soul. Yet at the same time Mama seemed afraid to give the Conjure Woman credit for anything.

Three days later, after drinking a good deal more tea, Rosalie declared, "Feelin' fine!"

Mama shook her head very hard and accused Rosalie of being a slave driver to herself.

"But there's work out there I got to do."

"Later," Mama said firmly. She'd been sitting beside her and reading aloud from the copy of the *North Star* that Hanna had taken from the church.

"But you heard what the preacher told us 'bout folks runnin'. There's more people than ever who got to get away to Canada."

"And you're among them," said Mama, closing the paper. "Everybody seems to know who you really are. Just as soon as you're ready to make the trip, I want you to take your son and head north. I'll help you memorize the line of stops to Rochester and the address of Mr. and Mrs. Post. They'll get you over into Canada. Promise me you'll go."

Rosalie sat up in the bed as if she were going to get out of it. "You don't listen, Dora. I tells you I got work to do."

"Then I'll do it with my husband."

Rosalie's feet touched the floor. "You know very well there's black people in hidin' all over now. Most of them won't trust no white woman who come lookin' for them. But I knows a hundred places they likely to be duckin' in at."

"So you're not going to listen to me?"

"No. I'm askin' you to listen to *me*. I needs the buckboard and some big empty flour sacks. Do wish we had old Johnny Appleseed 'stead of this new horse. What's her name? No, never mind, don't tell me. I'll feel bad enough if I has to whip her to get us away from somebody without I knows her name. Where is my clothes?"

"I hid them," said Mama.

"You did what? Listen here now, Dora. I'm older than you. Old enough to take you over my knee and spank you, like I was your aunt Ida. 'Specially when you behavin' like a spoiled child."

"All right, I'll give them to you. But just think of Rafe if not of yourself. What if something happens to you?"

"What's the matter with you? Look at the chances you done took with your little girl at your side. Leastways I'm going out by myself."

"Well, that was wrong. I realized that later."

"No, I don't think so. Ain't you learned yet, darlin', that we all takes our chances?"

Hanna stepped from behind the door, where she'd been hiding. "I'm goin' with Rosalie, Mama."

"No, you're not!"

"No, you ain't!"

"Don't you see, Mama? If anybody stops us, Rosalie can say she's takin' me somewhere. And I kin act like she's my nanny. Only I think we should do it in our new buggy. Rosalie, Papa says you're famous. And because of that new law, people are gonna be lookin' for you on this side of the river now."

A look of pride crossed Mama's face. "You are a brave girl," she said, running her fingers through Hanna's silky hair. "But I love you too much to involve you any more than I already have. Whatever has to be done, I will do it."

"No, you can't, Mama. Not like me. Everyone knows that Mother Freedom's workin' with a white woman. Papa's lawyer thinks the government people already know who both of you are. He says it's only a matter of time 'fore they come to the house with warrants."

"Why, you little scamp! You've been listening in at the bedroom door!"

"But I'm in this, too, Mama. I'm not a little girl anymore."

"No? How old, pray tell, do you feel you are?"

"I don't know. Not nine anyway."

"She makes sense," said Rosalie. "And they won't likely hurt her, bein' a white child and all."

"Unless the bullets fly," said Mama, and bit her lip. She was turning pale again.

"If she come 'long, I wouldn't let it get to that."

Suddenly Rafe ran screaming into the room and began punching Hanna in the side with his tiny fists.

Mama was too startled to do anything, but Rosalie flew across the room and grabbed his paper-thin arms.

"Take me, not her! You're *my* mammy!"

"Listen to me, darlin'. You gonna stay here with her mammy, just for awhile. And her mammy gonna teach you some more 'bout readin' and writin'. Then soon as I get the time, guess what?"

"What?" Rosalie had let go of his hands, and now he dried his eyes.

"You gonna teach me."

"But I don't want to learn to read and write!"

"You *don't*? Am I hearin' you straight? Don't you 'member that reverend sayin' the reason nobody will ever try to make him a slave is 'cause he's an educated man. Darlin', they are *afraid* of educated men and women. You are doin' your job for you and for me, too, by stayin' right here and learnin' everythin' you kin."

"Mammy, I wants to go to Canada. I don't wants to stay in that room down the ladder. I cain't see no daytime down there. I cain't see no outside. Even back to the squire's place I could look out the cabin door. I could go out an' feel the sunshine."

Rosalie's lips began to tremble. Her face ran with tears. She clutched him to herself. "Honey lamb, you breakin' my heart."

"Oh, don't cry, Mammy. I's sorry. I didn't mean to make you cry."

"You made *me* cry, too," declared Hanna, half seriously. "That hurt."

"Girl, you ain't hurt. If I done hit you the way I could hit you, why *then* you be hurt."

"Really? Let's see what you'd feel if I hit *you*."

"Hanna," said Mama sternly.

"Oh, they just playin' now," said Rosalie, bending to them. "They gettin' to be real good friends. Is I right?"

Rafe stared sourly at the floor. "Guess so."

Hanna stared sourly at the wall. "Guess so."

"Oh! I cannot tell you how happy I am," blurted Mama, "that I never had any brothers or sisters."

They went out three nights in a row without finding anyone. They took the road toward the river. And Rosalie's first stop each time was the old sawmill.

There was a pond behind it that was well-known to be good for fishing in the winter. And there was a tiny hut nearby that would be put into use when the water froze over solidly. Then it would be slid out into the middle of the pond. The hut had no floor, and so a small hole could be cut into the ice underneath it. Anyone in there could stay out of the wind while fishing.

The sawmill was closed at that hour. The old dog that had watched over it for years had died some months before and not been replaced. Rosalie thought this would be a good place to hide if someone was lucky enough to discover it. But she did not want to scare anyone by walking straight up to the place.

Getting out of the buggy a distance away from the sawmill, they moved up quietly and ducked behind a tall woodpile, where they could see one side of the hut.

Rosalie stared hard at it and thought it had been moved a bit closer to the water's edge.

"You got the eyesight, young'un. Look past the corner of it. See if you kin make out a line comin' out of it on the end of a stick."

Hanna stared hard. "Don't see a line. Too hard, Rosalie. It's some dark."

"What about a stick?"

"Think so. Might be. But I cain't be sure."

Rosalie gave her a little shove. "Your mama gonna blame me, you start talkin' like that again. Look at the water near there. See anythin' stirrin'?"

"I don't think I can reasonably be sure," Hanna replied in a mincing voice.

Rosalie gave her another shove. "This here is serious what we're doin'. Kin you whistle?"

"Well, you know I kin."

"Well, and you know I cain't. Whistle me 'Go

148

Down Moses in Egypt Land.' And keep your eye on that water right there in front. Loud now."

Hanna piped up. But she quickly stopped and pointed.

"There! Somebody pulled in a line. I saw it flash."

"Uh-huh. Someone mighty jumpy too." When Rosalie stood up, Hanna stood, too. "Not you, chile. Stay here and get ready to run if there's trouble. You don't never know who will turn out dangerous."

Hanna could see that Rosalie had her hand tucked inside the sleeve of her dress, where the pistol was hanging on a cord. She heard Rosalie singing that song of freedom softly as she walked toward the cabin. *Wove* toward it was more likely. Rosalie was acting drunk and Hanna understood why. Any black fugitive inside would pay attention to the freedom song. But what if, for some reason, one or two white men were in there? Mother Freedom didn't want to give herself away.

Hanna watched Rosalie turn the corner of the wall and disappear inside. She didn't like the awful stillness that followed. She could hear throbbing in her ears. She saw a man come out. He was very tall and wide in the shoulders, with long arms and big hands. But the rest of him was as thin as a string bean. He had what looked like bark tied around his feet, and wore pants that were not long enough to cover his ankles and a cotton shirt. His eyes darted this way and that, and fell upon Hanna.

"She a friend," said Rosalie, coming out after him.

He ducked his head but didn't say a word.

"I sure didn't count on anyone so big," Rosalie muttered to Hanna as he followed them to the buggy. "Don't see how I can fit him under the seat. I could get under it myself. But then I don't see how he could be ridin' with you. Not with what he got on! I didn't ask, but I 'spect he done somehow lost his clothes comin' over and took those off a scarecrow."

"So let me get under the seat, and he kin be your husband."

"That's a man I cain't even get to speak, and he's gonna be *my* husband?" Rosalie gave her a look. "Oh, I see. You don't think I'd give any husband of mine a chance to talk anyway." She burst out laughing.

It was good to see Rosalie happy again. There weren't many times Hanna did. But the smiles stopped just before they arrived at the crossroad that led back home. The road ahead was filled with men on horseback, galloping toward the hotel with rifles and flaming torches.

FIFTEEN

The new horse pulling the buggy was very young. She hadn't been all that comfortable being harnessed to the carriage in the first place. And when she saw those flames ahead, she whinnied, reared, and tried to back up.

One rider slowed down and looked their way. But the flame of his own torch made it harder for him to see beyond its light, and other horses coming behind him made him move on.

Even with Rosalie pulling at the reins, the mare was getting more and more out of control. Before she could whinny again, the silent man jumped down and took her by the halter. His strong hands pulled hard, but at the same time, he stared at her with a calming gaze. The horse was looking at him now rather than at the torches. He soothed her with a stroking hand and led the buggy off the road and into a stand of trees.

Touching Rosalie in the darkness, Hanna was amazed to feel her body trembling. Then all at once she understood.

"Rosalie, they won't find the secret room."

"You don't know that. Nobody knows that."

"Papa won't even let them in."

"He won't be able to do nothin' 'bout it if them men has warrants. They are goin' after my little boy to take him back to slavery. To be beaten. To be starved. And I cain't do nothin' to stop them."

Suddenly Rosalie said, "Wait! Yes, I can. It's really me they wants. I kin give myself up." She started for the road.

"Rosalie no! They'll kill you," Hanna cried.

The silent man sprang in front of her.

"Get out of my way, slave. You lookin' at a free woman here."

He shook his head and refused to budge.

"Listen," she said. "You don't need me. Just follow the Drinking Gourd. That will lead you north."

Again he shook his head.

"I'm finished tellin' you," she said, and pulled out her pistol.

The man refused to move.

Rosalie's arm dropped to her side. She began to cry.

"I'll get him out, Rosalie! I promise I will."

"You? How will you do it?"

"Through the tunnel."

"Tunnel ain't finished."

"Yes, it is! Don't you 'member? It was wide enough for me. I went through it already."

"No, you didn't. Some of it came down on you, and you thought you couldn't use your legs no more. You got turned around."

"Rosalie, I know I can make it. Please, you got to let me. It's what I came back for!"

"Came back? What you talkin' 'bout?"

"I don't know all of it. Somethin' the Conjure Woman reminded me of."

"Time like this you talkin' 'bout *dreams* again?"

The silent man gently put his hand on Rosalie's arm. It seemed to calm her. "How you gonna get past all of 'em?"

Hanna grew thoughtful. "They don't care 'bout *me*, Rosalie."

"You ain't thinkin' straight. When grown men gets all riled up 'bout catchin' and killin' anybody, they don't keep control on what's a-goin' on inside of 'em. But you too young to understand."

Hanna straightened up. "I'm older than I look, Rosalie."

"That again?"

"It's my *fate*, Rosalie."

"Fate? Don't know that word. What does that mean?"

"It means I can take care of myself."

"Oh sure you kin."

"Rosalie, it's the only way."

Tenderly, Mother Freedom touched her. "Anythin' happen to you . . . What do you think that would do to your mama and papa and me?"

"When we come through the tunnel, where do we go?"

"They gonna be on all the roads. They gonna surround the hotel 'fore they goes in. That's how it is with posses." Rosalie paused for a minute to think. "Best place to get to from the cemetery is the schoolteacher's cabin. He gone away. We meet there, God willin'. You see your folks, tell 'em how much I loves 'em."

Hanna kissed her and started to go.

"Hanna!"

"What?"

"I don't like this."

Hanna didn't like it either. And as soon as she was away from Rosalie, fear began to wash over her. Well, it was better not to think about that. Better to be like Mama. When Mama got scared, she just got all the more stubborn about what she wanted to do.

As she moved along in the darkness, Hanna tried to decide the best way to get to the hotel. She could try to sneak through the woods to the cemetery and go down into the tunnel to the secret room. But then she would be leaving a hole behind her that someone could find. They could be waiting there when she came back with Rafe.

The other choice was to keep going until she came to where the riders were and walk straight through them. She was going home, that's all. Yes, but what if they asked what she was doing out here so late by herself? Well, she'd sneaked out to see what the commotion was. All right, but what if they held on to her to make Mama and Papa do what they wanted— like give up Rafe? Or what if Rosalie was right to warn her about men who were "all riled up"?

"Hey, you!" a voice shouted at her.

It was one of the riders. She hadn't noticed him because he had no torch. He was off the road in the shadows with two other men, passing a jug.

In the darkness he couldn't see her well either. Should she run for it? Turning away suddenly, Hanna scooped up a handful of dirt and smeared her face with it. She would have torn a little rip in her pants, but there was no time for that.

"C'mere!" commanded the man. Hanna swaggered up to him, trying to make her voice sound boyish.

"Yes, suh! Kin I help you some?"

"Help?" said another man. "What kind of help, boy?"

"My pap, he sell good corn liquor. I go get it if y'all wants some."

"Where'all is your pap?"

"Back in there a ways. Drunk, though. So I'll get it for you."

Hanna started to turn away.

"Hold on there. You got girl's hair."

"Don't like bein' no girl," she said. "Girls got to stay home all the time and don't get to go a-huntin'."

"You kin hunt?"

"Yes, suh, shore kin."

"You don't look big enough to even hold a rifle."

"Let me have yourn and I'll show you."

"Don't think so. Might be you'd shoot me."

The men began to laugh. "Here now," one of them said, "how much for that corn liquor you're a-talkin' 'bout?"

Hanna had no idea what to say. "Well, I get it and you pay me what you think is right."

"Oh, I get it." One of the men chuckled. "You ain't gonna ask your pap how much 'cause he ain't gonna know 'bout it. Then when he wakes up, you gonna tell him he drunk it all hisself. Ain't that right?"

"You wouldn't tell on me, would you?"

"No, by thunder! We gonna do a right smart piece of business together. Best hurry now. We cain't stay here long."

"Be right back," Hanna said, darting into the woods.

As soon as she was gone, one of the men jumped out of the saddle. He was wearing moccasins instead of boots, and when his feet touched the ground, there wasn't a sound. Swiftly, the others followed him, keeping a distance behind Hanna.

Meanwhile, Hanna's eyes had grown used to the thick darkness of the woods. Moving more and more quickly, she headed for the cemetery. But each step took her closer to the ring of torches.

Falling to her knees, Hanna crawled along, trying to remember just where the barrel hoop that marked the entrance to the tunnel had been set in the ground. Several times her fingers dug into earth but she found only rocks and more earth below. Finally, one of her nails scraped against wood. Quickly, she cleared off the lid, lifted it, and slid down into the hole.

Hanna scuttled away from the opening as fast as she could. But the farther she went, the more strongly she began to feel that something was wrong. What could it be? Hanna struggled to remember.

But there was nothing she could think of. Hanna crawled on.

SIXTEEN

"Rafe, where are you?" she called, coming into pitch blackness.

"Here," he said, but she couldn't see him.

"Why's the lantern out?"

"Your mama she said to put it out. She don't want nothin' comin' from here. She say there are men fixin' to come into the hotel. Where's my mammy?"

"She sent me to come get you. You ready?"

"Girl, that ain't no kind of question. I was 'bout half ready to go by myself. Only how would I know where my mammy was at? Let's go."

But Hanna gropped for the ladder and started to climb. The feeling that something was terribly wrong was stronger than ever.

"What you doin'?"

"I have to see Mama and Papa."

"You crazy? You cain't go up there!"

"I got to! I have to say good-bye."

"What you sobbin' for? You gonna see them when you gets back."

"I won't! I know I won't see 'em again. Not ever!" Hanna had been pressing on the hatch but it wouldn't budge. "It won't open! Why won't it open?"

159

"'Cause they put somethin' over it to make it harder to find it, that's why."

She was pounding on the hatch now. "Rafe, help me. I've got to see them. Mama!" she screamed. "Mama! Let me come up! Oh Mama, please. I cain't go off like this."

She felt Rafe tugging at her foot. "Hanna, you listen. I'll go myself. You just tell me where my mammy is at."

Hanna hurried down and took his hands in hers. "Oh, you mean it? Would you? You'd go without me?" She wiped away her tears. "When you come out through the cemetery, you just turn to the right."

"Right is which?"

"It's this arm. No, *this* one. You understand? You go where this arm will be. Only that's if you climb out facin' front. 'Cause if you're facin' backward . . . oh, you won't get it!"

"You take me for a fool? Shore I will. This way if I come out front. That way if I come out back. What else?"

"Then you don't let anybody see you and keep goin' till you come to the schoolteacher's cabin."

"How long it take me?"

"I don't know. Not long. First you cross the creek. Well, the creek will be dry now, so you won't see any water there. But you go down it and then you go up the other side.

"The cabin is right near there. And there's a big water bucket in front of it." Hanna fell silent. "But if you get lost in the dark . . . "

"Shoot, I never gets lost in the dark. I'm goin'."

"Rafe are you sure?"

He didn't answer her. He was already in the tunnel.

Yes, he was gone. And suddenly it flashed upon her that it had happened this way before. That time, too, she'd felt horrible about letting him go off on his own. She'd gone after him, but it had been too late. Men hiding in the cemetery had watched him climb out of the tunnel—and they followed him. They stayed behind him until he found the dry creek. They'd ducked behind trees while he scrambled down the rocky bank and came up on the other side. They waited until he got turned around in the darkness . . . grew confused . . . and called out for his mammy. Waited a few seconds more until Rosalie appeared at the cabin door, a candle flickering in her hand.

And then they had shot her dead.

Hanna couldn't let it happen that way all over again! She had to stop it. She *could* stop it! Why else was she being given another chance? Crawling, praying, shouting, she plunged into the tunnel.

"Rafe, stop! Wait! Come back!"

He didn't answer.

SEVENTEEN

At the end of the long tunnel, Hanna lifted her head carefully and saw the backs of the three trackers. They were silently following Rafe.

Hanna opened her mouth to shout a warning, but nothing came from her throat. Was she afraid they would shoot Rafe if he started to run? Was she afraid they would shoot her? She didn't know what had gripped her throat. But this time Hanna didn't follow them.

She knew a different way to the cabin, a way that was more roundabout but faster. Cutting away from the men until she came to a meadow, Hanna bounded like a deer to another part of the creek. Her feet flew over the log bridge. Turning again, she dashed madly toward the schoolteacher's cabin.

There it was in the darkness, like a black lump under the high trees. Something was stirring nearby. Out of the corner of her eye she caught a glimpse of the silent man hidden away in the bushes with Papa's horse. Good! There was a chance for escape.

She was at the rear of the cabin now. There was no window to call through, and no time to get to the door. "Rosalie," she shouted through the back wall. "Get out of there quick! The slavers are comin'!"

Mother Freedom rushed outside, her pistol drawn. "Where's my Rafe?"

Hanna was panting hard. But still she heard loose stones falling. "He's down in the creek bed, tryin' to get here."

Rosalie cupped a hand to her mouth. "Rafe!" she boomed out. "Stay down there! Don't come up!"

Then she rushed toward the creek, shooting at the men who were coming out from behind the trees on the other side.

The silent man cracked a twig loudly. Hanna turned and he beckoned for her to come away with him. But she couldn't move from behind the cabin wall.

That other time the same thing had happened, but then it was while she was still behind those men. First her voice had gone, then her legs. All feeling in them had vanished as if they'd died underneath her. They were still killing Rosalie when she had crawled away. And she'd had no idea what had happened to Rafe.

But right now Rosalie was still alive and firing. She must have known that the men were too far away for her pistol shots to hit them. But it stopped them from coming any closer to the deep slope of the creek. Instead they took up positions and fired their rifles. Hanna saw Rosalie fall . . . saw her get up and shoot again.

And this time Hanna was on her feet, racing like the wind for the creek. Before the men could turn their rifles on her, she was sliding feet first down the rocky bank.

Rafe had fallen, stunned by a rock that had come crashing down on his head. She tugged his arm and pulled him up. He was bleeding and confused, and didn't seem to know where he was or even who he was. But she made him stumble along beside her.

Behind her she heard men screaming for joy. "We got her! We got her. We get the reward!"

"String her up first. Then we'll take her back!"

"What are you talkin' 'bout? She's already deader'n a fence post."

"Hang her anyways!"

"Hold on, fellers. We're forgettin' 'bout the boy. Gonna make some reward money on him, too, ain't we? Lessen we want to keep him private like for ourselves, 'stead of returnin' him."

"Figure that one out later! Let's get him! Where is he?"

"Beats me. I thought he went down here in the creek bed. Now I don't see hide nor hair of him. And that was a girl who just climbed down after him, wasn't it? 'Peared like the one we followed 'fore to that tunnel."

"Well now. We better hope we didn't shoot *her* up none. Nobody put up no reward for pluggin' no *white* folks. We could be arrested ourselves for that one, boys."

"I 'spect we got troubles then," said the man sliding

down the creek bank. "Look at this here rock. Got blood on it. Might be we shot her."

"You know what? We'd best finish both of 'em off and dump 'em somewhere. We won't say nothin' to nobody 'bout findin' that tunnel, just 'bout trackin' down the woman. That'd be the safest thing for us to do. Fan out, boys, and go down both sides of this creek till we get 'em."

But the children, hand in hand, were running . . . running . . . running. Hanna blinked. The creek bed was disappearing ahead of them into a great mist. "Rafe, faster!"

From behind came shouting. "I see 'em, boys! There they are. Shoot!"

The blood flowing down Rafe's forehead made it hard for him to see where he was going. Stumbling over a large rock, he tripped and fell to the side. Hanna fell with him just as rifle fire crackled overhead.

Then they were on their feet and running again.

The trackers were running, too. There was another burst of gunfire as the children plunged into the mist.

They were in rain . . . hissing, drenching rain. Roaring noises came out of the darkness, and two great lamps came hurtling toward them at tremendous speed. There was a loud warning blare. But Rafe, standing there wiping the streaming blood from his eyes, had no idea what was happening. Anna yanked him out of the way . . . and a huge eighteen-wheeler truck thundered by.

Anna looked around in amazement. They were in the middle of a highway with nighttime traffic thundering past in both directions.

She pulled Rafe across to the side of the road, but Rafe couldn't stop staring at the huge mechanical monsters. "Wha . . . what is all that?"

"They're machines, Rafe. Like the railroad engines, only they don't run on tracks. But they're just as dangerous if you stand in front of them."

"Why ain't I never heard of 'em 'fore? And where is we?"

"Rafe, I know this is going to be hard for you to understand, but we've skipped ahead in time. This is years and years and years later. People have been born and have had grandchildren and died since then."

He was looking strangely at her now, and suddenly he yanked his hand from hers. "Who is you?"

"What are you talking about? You know who I am. I'm Anna."

He jumped back. "Hanna? No, you ain't!"

"Look, you hurt your head. You're not seeing right."

"And I'm tellin' you, you too *big* for Hanna! And your voice done changed. And . . . and you ain't even wearin' the same . . . What that on you feet?"

She looked down. "Sneakers."

"Sneakers? What is that?"

"Listen to me, Rafe. I'm trying to explain to you what's happened."

"All I wants to know is: Where's my mammy? How I get back there? I wants to get back to my mammy."

"Oh, Rafe! She's . . . Rafe, she . . . I'm so sorry, Rafe . . . but . . ."

"They done killed my mammy? That what you sayin'? They done killed her?"

Anna began to tremble. "I saw they were following you," she blurted, "and I tried to get there first to warn her. But she wouldn't run away because she wanted to stop them from getting you, and—"

"I goin' back! I goin' back to be with my mammy."

"Rafe, listen to me. I was safe here already. You're the reason I went back to the past. It was to skip you ahead so *you'd* be safe!"

"Then . . . *I* go back to the past like you done, and I skips her over!"

"But you can't. It's too late. She's dead, don't you see? She's been dead over a hundred and forty years. We're in another time. Another place."

"I don't care! You go back! You go back right now to get my mammy. And I go with you. How'd you do it 'fore?"

"I . . . went back through the tunnel."

"Then I finds that tunnel and I goes back through it."

"But we can't do that now. We don't even know where we are."

"Yes, we do! We close to the creek. We just done left it!"

"Then those men will shoot us down!"

"Maybe they be gone time we get back."

"Then she'd be dead already, Rafe. Don't you understand that?"

"No! I don't understand nothin'!" he said. Veering away from her, he dashed headlong into the onrushing traffic and stopped in the middle of it. He stood there confused, peering into the darkness.

"Hanna!" he cried. "I don't see it! Where's it at? Where's that fog?"

"Rafe! Watch out! You can't stay there! No, wait a minute! Don't move. I'll come get you."

But he was already racing away. "There it is!"

A screeching car nearly went off the highway to avoid hitting him. Anna saw him reach the other side of the road, but a speeding convoy of trucks blocked her path. As soon as she could cross, she went after him. Only where was he? Had he actually found the fog and disappeared into it? Had he gone back for Rosalie?

Anna's slowing footsteps brought her up a driveway to a dark shopping mall. There was nothing here but a long, rambling building. She went all the way around it looking for Rafe. Then she noticed the field.

No lights from the road reached back here, and it was very dark beneath the starless sky. Yet in the distance, she could make out the outlines of a cabin. She called out to Rafe, but there was no answer.

A wild hope opened up in Anna's mind. Maybe Rafe had the right idea. What if there really was a chance to return again, early enough this time to save Rosalie? She started to run. The high weeds and wild grass made it impossible to see where her feet were going. One of them turned on a rock. She felt something tearing. There was a shock of pain, and down she went.

She lay in the grass, her ankle throbbing. Then she heard Rafe's moaning cry, "Oh, Mammy, where is you? Mammy, please don't leave me. I loves you so, Mammy. Oh, why won't you let me find where you is?"

Anna tried to stand, but halfway to her feet she went down again. On her hands and knees, she crawled to Rafe through the soaking wet grass, the weeds, the cornflowers.

The rain had stopped by the time she reached him. Rafe was sitting against a part of the tumbled-down shack that was still standing. He turned his head so she wouldn't see he'd been crying, and the first time she tried to hold him he pulled away.

She moved back to give him room. At last she said, "You know what I think, Li'l Rafe."

"I'm not Li'l Rafe. I'm *Rafe*."

"You're right. I'm sorry. I think your mother would have been very glad you came with me."

"Does you think so?" he asked in a tiny voice.

"Yes, truly I do," Anna said, falling silent for a moment. "And I'll tell you something else. What just happened to us—coming here into another time—is a miracle. There has to be a reason for it."

"Then why wasn't there a miracle for my mammy?" he demanded.

"I'm not sure," Anna said, and grew thoughtful. "Maybe it's that the work she had to do was back then. But when we grow up, we'll tell the whole world about her, won't we, Rafe?"

He fought back the brimming tears. "No, *I'll* do it!"

"You won't let me help you . . . like Mama helped Mother Freedom?"

He brushed his eyes with the back of his hand. "I guess so."

"Good! And then we'll try to do the things they would have done if they were living now. Does that sound all right?"

Rafe could only nod. It was all he could do to keep from sobbing out loud. But if Anna was still his friend, maybe he could let her be there if he wanted to cry.

He did want to—very badly. So did Anna. And when she had wrapped her arms around him, they both wept.

171

EIGHTEEN

Every day for a whole week Kevin Post had been squatting gloomily on the top step of the hotel porch, waiting for his big sister to show up. Finally, he turned to his parents, who were numbly sitting in their rocking chairs.

"Maybe we're waiting in the wrong place."

"What, Kevin?" his mother said absently.

"I bet Anna will come back somewhere else."

His father sat up a little taller. "Why do you say that, Kev?"

"'Cause this is where she *leaves* from, Dad."

"I don't get—"

Kevin's mother suddenly jumped to her feet. "Allan, he's right. This isn't the place where we found her!"

"Wait a minute, Barb. Are you saying . . . ?"

"We have to go back to that field where we first saw her!"

In almost no time they were on the road, heading for the airport. The man they returned their rented minivan to wanted to take forever adding up the bill. Allan just tossed him the keys and ran off, shouting "I'll be in touch." The woman at the airline ticket counter was sorry, but there just weren't three seats on the next plane out. Barb paid some teenagers fifty dollars each to switch to the next flight. The jet was late taking off and later still setting down, and even then, they were only as far as New York City. They still had to take another plane to Rochester!

It was very late at night by the time they arrived and were back in their own car. Then came another problem. It had been three years since the Posts had driven on the road where they had stopped to pick cornflowers. Things had changed. The road had been widened, and all sorts of new buildings had gone up: stores, gas stations . . .

Suddenly, Barb tapped her husband's arm. "Allan, turn here. Turn right."

"What? Into a shopping—"

"Please, just do it!"

"You saw something?" he asked, as they pulled into the parking lot of a mall.

"Don't stop here. Go around the building."

As the car circled the mall, its headlights lit up part of a field. Barb pointed. "Look, Allan."

"Honey." He sighed. "We'll probably find these same wildflowers all over the—"

"No, look out there. Isn't that a cabin?"

Allan squinted into the shadows made by the car's headlights. "You're right!"

The first to spring out of the car was Kevin. He ran

ahead, and if it wasn't for his waving arms, they'd have lost sight of him in the tall weeds. "Anna! Anna!" he cried.

They heard another voice, calling his name. And then they saw her.

"Look! Look, Allan!" Barb panted breathlessly. "She's standing! Do you see her standing?"

"Yes, of course I see it!"

Anna took one step away from the cabin wall and sank down. But a moment later she was up again, leaning on someone. It was a boy about their son's age.

The Posts watched Kevin dash out of the weeds and fling his arms around his sister. Catching up with him moments later, everyone was laughing and crying at the same time.

But something was nagging at Anna, and it kept her from showing just how glad she was that the Posts had found her. She could tell that they were starting to sense it, too, and that upset her even more.

"Let's not crowd her," suggested Allan. There was a confused and painful silence, until he said softly, "Listen to me, please, darling. We don't know yet what you've been through. We may never understand it completely. But there's one thing we want you to know—"

Barb interrupted eagerly. "We are so grateful you've come back to us. Thank you. Thank you for that!"

"And, Anna," Allan put in, "we know that things had to change once you found your real par—well, we feel we're also your real—well, we're your family, too! Now! In *this* world! But . . . but what we want to say is—"

"They're trying to tell you," Kevin jumped in, "that it's okay if you love a couple of ghosts."

"That's not how your father meant it!" said Barb, glaring at him. "But, Anna, you don't have to give up anything you feel you found or . . . "

Anna felt her chest begin to lighten. She took a few steps by herself and threw herself into their arms.

Moments later she reached out for the boy standing alone by the wall. "This is my very best friend in the world, Rafe Sims," she said, knowing that both of them had at last come to the end of their journey.